A Night in Distant Motion

A Night in Distant Motion

a novel by Irina Korschunow

translated by Leigh Hafrey

DAVID R. GODINE · *Publisher*
BOSTON

First published in English in 1983 by

DAVID R. GODINE, PUBLISHER, INC.
306 Dartmouth Street
Boston, Massachusetts 02116

Copyright © 1979 Benziger Verlag Zürich, Köln
Translation copyright © 1983 by Leigh Hafrey

Library of Congress Cataloging in Publication Data

Korschunow, Irina.
    A night in distant motion.

    Translation of: Er Hiess Jan.
    Summary: When seventeen-year-old Regine, a Nazi supporter, falls in love with a Polish prisoner in 1944, she notices for the first time the injustices and horrors going on around her and discovers she can no longer be silent.
    1. World War, 1939-1945 – Germany – Juvenile fiction.
    [1. World War, 1939-1945 – Germany – Fiction.
    2. Germany – History – 1933-1945 – Fiction] I. Title.
    PZ7.K8376Hi 1982   [Fic]   81-47325
    ISBN 0-87923-399-0   AACR2

First edition

Printed in the United States of America

Translator's Note

In translating the following story, I have left refer-
ences to certain aspects of daily life in Germany
during the 1930s and 1940s unchanged: American
readers will remember that one meter = 3.2 feet,
that one kilogram = 2.2 pounds, and that one ki-
lometer = .6 miles. The German system of academic
grading referred to in the text runs from one to six,
with one the highest and six the lowest grade.

 A number of abbreviations or acronyms also occur
in the book, mostly with reference to military and
political conditions prevailing in Germany just before and during World War II. 'POW' stands for
'prisoner of war.' 'NS' is a short form of the acronym
NSDAP (*Nationalsozialistische Deutsche Arbeiterpartei*)
or National Socialist German Workers' party, the
party of which Adolf Hitler, periodically referred to
in the following pages as the '*Führer*' (leader), was
the head. The slang term '*Sozi*' referred to the Social
Democrat party in Germany, a party that opposed

the National Socialists and that was suppressed when Hitler came to power in 1933. Arms of the National Socialist party mentioned in the text are: the 'ss' or *Schutzstaffel*, an elite political, paramilitary group, identifiable by the members' black uniforms; the 'sa' or *Sturmabteilung*, the storm troops referred to in the text as 'brown shirts'; and the 'GESTAPO' or *Geheime Staatspolizei*, which functioned as a political police force. Finally, the *Hitler Jugend* or Hitler Youth, with the subdivision called the German Girls' League, had party-oriented educational functions indicated by their English names.

A word on pronunciation: Most of the names in the text can safely be pronounced as they would be in English. The two exceptions are 'Jan,' which should be pronounced 'Yahn'; and 'Regine,' which has a hard *g* (as in *gh*ost) and takes a slight emphasis on the final, short *e* (as in lock*e*t), thus: Reghíne.

LEIGH HAFREY
December 1981

A Night in Distant Motion

Chapter One

EIGHT square meters, no more. Four white walls, a window, a bed, a table, a chair, a stove . . . 'Go up to the attic,' the farmer's wife said when I knocked on her door that night and asked if she could hide me.

She stood in the hall, a candle stub in her hand. The gray braid fell across her left shoulder. Her nightgown was gray, too. Until then I had only seen her in black: black dress, black apron, black kerchief. I had never imagined a braid under her kerchief.

Now I saw nothing but that braid.

'Go up to the attic,' said the farmer's wife.

I felt her hand on my arm. She pushed me to the stairs, led me up the narrow, worn steps, pushed me through the door. I let myself fall on the bed. I had run twenty-seven kilometers. Twenty-seven kilometers in three hours.

'Sleep, Regine,' said the farmer's wife and covered me. First light was coming in at the window. The gray braid swayed before my eyes.

That was in October. I've been here since then.

At first I thought I wouldn't make it. To be shut in, unable to leave, to be afraid that the door would open, that they'd come for me, seize me, drag me off. When it got dark and I sat there without a light, I wanted to jump up, scream, bang my head against the wall.

Since then I've learned there's only one thing: waiting.

Why did it all happen this way?

I sit in the attic at Henninghof and think it over. I think, think, think. I'm afraid and then I think and then I'm afraid. Below lies the village street. I've pulled my chair up to the window, but not right up, just enough so I can look out without being seen from the street. The white muslin curtains help to hide me, and Henninghof lies at the edge of the village, with nothing across the street. But I sit on the edge of my chair, always ready to run, though I can't imagine where. Me, me of all people.

Jan once said: 'You have to hold completely still. Then it all passes over more easily, one way or another.'

Maurice says: 'Think, *ma petite,* now you have the time. He who thinks, learns. And when you get out of here, show what you've learned.'

But will I ever get out again? Sometimes I think this must be eternity. Just this attic forever and ever. The view from the window. Snow covers the cobblestones, gray and slushy from the carts going out to manure the fields. The hoofbeats of the horses, the rattle of the ironbound wheels are virtually the only sounds now, in January.

I know they drive by and no one lifts his head. Still, when I hear one of the carts, I press against the wall and my palms go damp with fear. Did the woman or the old man on the box see my shadow against the curtains? Will they report it? Will they betray me?

Denunciation is your duty.

One is punished if one doesn't comply.

That always seemed right to me, earlier, in the time before Jan. But perhaps people are different here in Gutwegen, in this small village so far from the city, with heath and forest all around and nothing but their work. Even during summer vacation, when I volunteered for the harvest, I was surprised at how little they bother with regulations. ' Day,' they said, instead of '*Heil* Hitler,' 'Mornin',' 'Evenin',' and from the beginning they let the French POWs who work for them sit at the same table.

One of them often sits up on the muck cart, although they're forbidden to leave the farmyard un-

5

accompanied. But all the men except the old ones are either at the front or wounded or dead, and there has to be someone to do the work.

'They can't assign a guard to each and every one of us,' says Maurice. 'And they don't need to. We won't run away, not now that the war is almost over.'

Maurice has been at Henninghof more than two years now. He lives in the room over the stable, because POWs and Germans aren't allowed to sleep under the same roof. But otherwise he moves about the house as though he belonged here. Everyday Sergeant Kropp comes by on his rounds, leans his bike against the side of the barn, has some bread and sausage in the kitchen, and moves on. As long as Maurice stays put, it's all right.

I can't believe that still upset me last summer.

I recall the day we mowed the oats; the stalks lay on the ground after the storm and the reaper blades couldn't cut them. Maurice swung his scythe across the field, Gertrud and I followed and bound the sheaves, morning to noon at the same steady pace. Then we sat under the linden tree. The farmer's wife had given us sandwiches and coffee, we were tired and sweaty, and there was only one cup.

Maurice drinks, Gertrud drinks. She offers me the mug. I shake my head.

'Aren't you thirsty?' Gertrud asks.

I shake my head again.

'I see,' she says.

'Couldn't your mother have packed two mugs?' I ask.

'She's got other things on her mind,' says Gertrud, and I fall silent.

'You can report it,' says Gertrud.

She looks at me with her cold gaze, and I feel small and foolish next to her, even though she's only nine years older, twenty-six.

She drinks again, gives me the mug, and I drink, too.

By that time three of her brothers had already been killed, and the farmer's wife looked as numb and dark as one of the carved figures in our cathedral. I took the mug because of her. But I only spoke to Maurice when it was absolutely necessary, and at the table I acted as though he weren't there.

When was that? Just six months ago? Now they're my friends, Gertrud and Maurice, and have been from the first morning here in the attic.

The first morning after that terrible night. I was sleeping; the door opened, I awoke, started, jumped out of bed . . .

'It's only me,' said Gertrud.

She stood in the doorway, a tray in her hand.

'What ever have they done to you?' she asked.

She carried the tray to the table, poured me some malt coffee, spread drippings on a slab of bread.

'Eat now,' she said. 'It helps.'

I was hungry and afraid and I swallowed the bread half-chewed. Gertrud stood on the other side of the table and watched me, with a changed look in her eyes, almost the way she looks at calves when she gives them milk.

'Mother has told me everything,' she said. 'You're safe up here.'

Later Maurice came and brought wood. The stove hadn't been used in years. Maurice cleaned it, took off the pipe, knocked the hard-baked soot out of the elbow, and put it back together. He worked in silence. Only when the fire had caught did he turn to me.

'Now it'll warm up, *ma petite*,' he said.

Ma petite. That's what he has called me since that morning.

'You don't have to worry. Time passes. The war won't last much longer.'

He looked at my shorn head and scorched hair.

'That will grow back, too.'

I said, 'Thanks, Maurice.'

I was ashamed.

No, they won't betray me, neither the farmer's wife, nor Gertrud, nor Maurice. In the evening, when the doors are locked and the windows blacked out, I go down to them, and we sit around the big table. The farmer's wife folds her hands in her lap; black and silently she looks at the five pictures that hang over the sofa – her husband and her four sons. None is alive now. The farmer died in 1943, one son after another has fallen: the first right at the beginning in Poland, the second at Stalingrad, the third in France when the Americans and the British landed, the fourth last September, somewhere on the eastern front. Walter, the youngest, whom I knew.

The farmer's wife sits there and looks at them. Her glance always returns to them. Sometimes she reads the Bible, mostly psalms, out loud. I think that's the only way she can read. 'Blessed the man who walks not in the valley of the wicked, nor loiters on the way that sinners take . . . O Lord my God, in thee do I take refuge; from all my pursuers save me, and deliver me . . .'

Her words fall into the conversation between Maurice, Gertrud, and me: The war, the war, always the war. At eight there's the news from the German radio, army communiqués, rallying cries. And later Radio London. German-language news broadcasts from England – just last summer I didn't know there was such a thing. Maurice turns the radio on very low, so that we have to press our ears to the speaker. Only the farmer's wife stands at the window. She listens for the creak of the gate, the dog's bark, the crunch of steps on the gravel. If someone comes, we have to turn off the radio. Just listening to enemy broadcasts is punishable by death.

So many things draw the death penalty now. At the baker's, if you say 'Why doesn't Hitler put an end to his damned war?' they hang you straight off. Perhaps even if you do what I did. And if you hide someone like me.

'Death is a lot cheaper than cabbages here,' says Maurice.

I sit in the attic. It is January, the last week of January 1945. The snow lies on the village street, and London says the war is coming to an end. The Americans have already passed Aachen, the Russians have advanced into Silesia, and I sit up here and wait for it all to be over. For us finally to have lost the war.

I *want* us to lose, though I dread the end. What will our victors do to us? Everyone hates us. We've done so much to them, and they will take their revenge. But if we lose the war, I can go home. I can find out if Jan is still alive. Maybe I can see him again.

I want us to lose the war. Four months ago – if I had heard those words somewhere four months ago, I would have gone to the police. A traitor. Someone who will stab us in the back, our soldiers, our homeland, our *Führer*. I would have reported it, even four months ago. My name was Regine Martens then, too; I had blond hair, gray eyes, stood five foot two, slim, with heavy legs. The same as now. But even the way I look isn't quite right anymore. My hair has grown back, it already covers my ears, but still I look different. Maybe it's because everything else has changed, my whole life, and if

I had sensed that when it began – the twelfth of September – I would probably have crawled into bed and pulled the blanket over my head. No, not even that. I wouldn't have believed it. I would have laughed, shrugged my shoulders. Because I was still the other Regine Martens and couldn't imagine that I would fall in love with someone like Jan.

Jan. I say his name to myself and think, he has to come in through that door and stand before me, tall, his shoulders drooping forward a bit, with his lank hair and those very clear eyes. Has to come in, look at me, stretch out his hands to me.

But he won't come.

Chapter Two

THE twelfth of September, my birthday.

'Sleep well,' my mother had said the preceding evening. 'Tomorrow you'll be seventeen. I hope there won't be an air alert. Have you packed your case?'

Our air-raid kit stood ready in the hall closet. But every evening before she went to sleep, she asked: 'Have you packed your case?'

It got on my nerves. Her snoring also got on my nerves. I lay next to her and thought, if my father had been an engineer or a chemist instead of a bookkeeper, they wouldn't have sent him to the front. The cannery would have declared him indispensable, like Dr. Hagemann and Mr. Franke and the two Lieberechts; and I could be lying in my room instead of here in my parents' bed next to my mother, who can't bear to sleep alone since my father was reported missing in action in Russia.

The sirens went off shortly after twelve.

'Get up, Regine,' my mother said and pulled the covers off me. 'They're headed for Berlin again.'

'Nothing will happen to us anyway,' I said.

'Hurry up,' said my mother. 'Otherwise Feldmann will come.'

'He needs some fun, too,' I said. I still found Feldmann amusing then, especially as an air-raid warden, running through the house yelling 'To the cellar! To the cellar!' Everyone came of his own accord anyway; you didn't dare call your own tune in a building full of company apartments. And the men had to stand by for fire duty – the machine engineer, the chemist, the foremen.

'It's only right,' my mother said. 'If they aren't at the front, the least they can do is see to it the factory doesn't burn down.'

Feldmann had only been deferred from the army because of a damaged hip. He limped, worked as an office messenger, lived in the basement apartment, and had to greet everyone in the building. '*Heil* Hitler!' he would call out from a distance, raising his hand and at the same time bowing. His sheer servility made him more and more twisted. During air alerts, though, he took on the voice of authority and yelled at whoever violated regulations, even Dr. Hagemann. We found him ridiculous, but still feared him. I'm almost certain it was he who denounced me. But I don't know for sure. Maybe it was someone else, one of the really nice people in the building. Maybe someone who had smiled at me the day before and whom I can't imagine could have been the cause of everything that has happened.

As we went down the basement stairs, the enemy bombers were already roaring overhead. I wasn't worried, though. Our city had never been attacked.

'Those poor Berliners,' my mother said. 'Or are they flying against Magdeburg today?'

Everyone had already gathered below – the Hagemanns, the Frankes, Mrs. Kunowski, the three Lieberechts, Mrs. Bühler, Mrs. Albrecht with her twins, the Feldmanns, and old Mrs. Schulz, who had kept house for her grandson but didn't bother to after he was killed; it had reached the point now where it smelled outside her door. I see them sitting in the basement, each in his place, nodding to us and exchanging a word or two. We'd been acquainted a long time, knew all about each other, wished each other well on birthdays. My mother had a calendar hanging in the kitchen specially, so she wouldn't forget anyone. Naturally there was also a lot of gossip. At the time, everyone was up in arms about old Mrs. Schulz. But the women in the building still shopped for her and by turns brought her something warm for lunch. All in all, very decent people.

One of them must have done it.

'Attach face masks!' Feldmann ordered, just as we sat down.

'That's really unnecessary, as long as nothing's happening,' complained Mrs. Albrecht. 'You can barely breathe with these things on.'

She obeyed, though, just like the others.

I had to laugh. We looked so funny, with damp cloths over mouth and chin and wide-open eyes.

'What's so funny?' Feldmann snuffled behind his mask, and I snuffled back: 'Laughing is allowed, Mr. Feldmann. Laughing is healthy.' My mother dug her elbow into my side and shook her head warningly.

And then it began.

First there was a hissing and screaming. 'Parachute mines!' someone yelled. Then there was an explosion. I saw one of the columns in the basement tremble. There was another explosion, and a black crack ran across the whitewashed ceiling. Plaster fell from the walls, the light flickered and went out, my nostrils and eyes were filled with dust.

We all screamed. My mother grabbed my arm. To the right in front of me sat Feldmann's oldest son, a thin boy, eight or so, who stuttered and couldn't look you in the face, just like his father. His mother had died three years ago; Feldmann's new wife had two small children of her own, and she was holding them in her lap. She ignored the boy.

When the second bomb fell, he stretched out his hand to me. I put an arm around him, and he crept up close. We crouched there, my mother, the boy, and I, holding tight and breathing together. There was a whistle, an explosion. The ground shook and we thought, now the ceiling will fall in and it'll all be over.

Then it stopped. Silence fell. A strange silence. Until the sirens went off again. All clear.

Feldmann switched on his flashlight.

'Let's go!' he bellowed. 'Franke and Hagemann up top, look for incendiary bombs. Everyone else out for fire fighting!'

We ran into the open air. A smell of burning met us – smoke, soot, dust. I was glad to have the face mask.

The cannery had taken a number of hits. The administration building, the engine room, the warehouse – nothing now but heaps of rubble, from which a red wall of flame rose in the night.

The Polish workers' barracks was also burning. The Poles stood in the courtyard, wrapped in blankets, some only in underwear. There was no air-raid shelter for them. They had probably all been sleeping when the bombing began.

Injured people lay on the ground. One of them, an older man, had a large wound in his arm. A young man crouched next to him. He looked at my first-aid kit.

'Help him. Please!' he said.

I didn't know what to do. It was the first injured person I had seen, with the first real blood. And a Pole besides. One of those subhumans.

Subhumans. Jews, Poles, Russians – all subhuman. Did I really believe that? I think of Jan. His eyes. His hands. His voice. The things he said.

'I don't want to hate,' he said once. 'There's so much hatred in the world. I don't want to add to it. I want there to be less of it.' But on the night of the bombs, when I had to bandage the Pole, I thought the word: subhuman. I wanted to turn and walk away.

The injured man moaned. His face was gray. 'Do help! Please!' the other repeated.

He had a strange voice. Husky, hoarse. And yet soft. I can't think of any other word. Soft.

I opened my kit, and Lisabeth Hagemann, who was standing next to me, exclaimed: 'You aren't going to help the Polacks!' She was three years older than I. We had played together once. Now she worked in the office and was engaged to a lieutenant.

She pointed toward the fire. 'They're to blame for that. Don't touch them!'

She was actually screaming. Her face was all twisted.

She grabbed my arm and tried to pull me away, and suddenly I wanted to help the Pole. Mrs. Bühler came to my aid.

'Those people work for us,' she said. 'Of course we have to take care of them.'

Mrs. Bühler of all people. I still remember how surprised I was. Her husband had gone to Poland in 1940 to take over the administration of a number of canneries. 'A crackerjack, Bühler,' my father had said. 'He'll bring the Polacks in line.' His wife said he lived in a villa with two maids. She was to follow.

But just before her departure he was murdered by Polish partisans. And now she wanted to help a Pole. I couldn't understand it. But it was fine with me because of Lisabeth Hagemann. I knelt next to the man, stopped the bleeding, and put muslin on the wound. I felt sick when I saw the raw, bloody flesh. The man screamed. As I bandaged him, the other held his head. 'Thanks,' he said, again with that strange voice.

I didn't answer. I didn't know yet that it was Jan.

The clock struck four as we got back to the apartment – filthy, tired, eyes burning. My hair sticky with soot.

The house was intact. But the windowpanes of the dining room, the kitchen, and the bathroom, all of which faced the factory, had been shattered by the explosions. The panes of the breakfront, the glasses and carafes that had stood in it, were all broken, lamps on the floor, pictures, plaster.

My mother stood in the door and looked silently at the pieces. Her apartment had always been sacred to her. I thought she'd start right in cleaning, but she said: 'I'm exhausted. Let's leave everything until morning.'

Then she took me in her arms and kissed me.

'It's your birthday. Best wishes. I hope Papa comes back this year.'

She was crying. She cried so often lately. It hadn't been that way before. And she also hadn't hugged me since my childhood. It wasn't usual for us, nor for my mother and grandmother. I had often wanted a little tenderness. And now it was almost unpleasant to feel her big, soft chest and her belly.

'Go lie down, Mama,' I said. 'I'm coming.'

Through the bedroom door I heard her, still crying. I heard her undress and get into bed, heard silence fall. Whether she's happy or sad, my mother goes to sleep immediately after she has tucked herself in.

I went into my room, which looks out on the gardens, and I opened the window. There was a smell of burning again, but no fire in sight. It was a black night, no moon, no stars. Only the searchlight beams wandered across the sky.

My birthday. This was my birthday. Seventeen years old. Parachute mines, bombs, fear. But I was still alive. I had bandaged someone and put out a fire. Such strange feelings as I looked out into the night. I'm not afraid anymore; I'm alive, I'll live on, many days, one day after another; the time will come, something will come for which I'm waiting. I stand at the window and breathe and am alive; everything is horrible, but I'm happy in the night.

Yes, that's how it was.

Chapter Three

THE next morning I didn't go to school. We slept late, washed, and began to clean up. I was just nailing pasteboard to the empty window frames when my grandmother arrived. First she hung her dark-blue coat on a hanger and put on an apron. Then she went into the dining room. She stood among the shards of glass with tight-pressed lips.

'And the sideboard's had a corner knocked off,' she said reproachfully, as though my mother were to blame. 'A good thing Father hasn't lived to see this.'

I almost laughed. My grandfather had made the sideboard himself, but I'm sure he would have found the comment amusing.

We learned from my grandmother that some fifty people had been killed in the city. Fifty. Not many compared with Berlin, Hannover, Munich, the Ruhr. But the first dead here. Steinbergen, thirty thousand inhabitants, no raids until now.

I took my bike and rode through the streets. Two sisters in my class had lived in one of the destroyed houses. They lay under the ruins. The old butcher, Sachse, who returned to his shop at the beginning of the war, had died along with his daughter-in-law and grandson. And the cobbler in the rear building, cobbler Furchtmann, whom I had so enjoyed visiting. He always sat at a table by the kitchen window. His gleaming cobbler's globe hung from the ceiling and refracted the light. He told me stories about the globe, and I was allowed to hammer nails through bits of leather. Now he was dead and his globe smashed.

Then I stood in front of the cathedral. In front of the heap of rubble they had left behind. Our cathedral, the Steinbergen cathedral, in North German brick-Gothic style. I had passed it every day and hardly noticed it anymore. The cathedral had been there, though, and now it wasn't anymore.

'Those pigs!' said a man standing beside me. 'Goddamned bastards! If we just had one of them. I'd put my foot in his face.' He's right, I thought.

And that afternoon, I ran into Jan again.

'See if you can get some vegetables from Steffens,' my mother had said in the afternoon. 'Carrots. Or beets. Tell him it's your birthday. Maybe he'll give you white cabbage.'

I didn't want to go, although it was only a little way to the truck garden. I couldn't stand old Steffens, with his red face and big belly. He always came too close, patted my cheek, and put his arm around my shoulders, reeking of onions and schnapps. He didn't do it to my mother, but then she didn't get any vegetables.

'Do go!' my mother pleaded. 'Maybe he'll even throw in a couple of eggs.'

Sometimes he did, in fact, give me eggs. He had everything, the old beast, not just the vegetable garden, but a farm, cows, chickens . . .

That's how I saw it then. Later, when he became our friend, I regretted it.

The twelfth of September, my birthday, the day after the night of the bombs.

'Mr. Steffens!' I call, and walk down the length of the greenhouses. 'Mr. Steffens!'

A man comes out of the shed. He's young. He has on blue overalls. There's a letter sewn on the breast. *P* for Pole. The symbol all Polish workers have to wear, so you know with whom you're dealing.

'Mr. Steffens will be back in an hour,' he says, and I recognize the voice. He looks at me with his clear eyes. It's quiet in the garden.

'How is your friend?' I ask, and don't know why I'm talking with the Pole.

'They took him away,' he says.

'Where to?' I ask. 'To the hospital?'

'Somewhere,' he says, and shrugs his shoulders.

'Can you visit him?' I ask.

'Visit him? Me?' He lowers his head, pushes weeds aside with his foot. Then he looks at me again and smiles.

'Thank you for helping him. It's good for people to help each other. People wearing a P, people without it.'

Neither of us speaks for a bit.

'Where did you learn such good German?' I ask.

'I grew up near the border,' he says. 'The Poles speak German there, and the Germans speak Polish.'

We fall silent again. Asters bloom among the garden beds. Light and shadow play across the walk.

'How is it you work here?' I ask. 'You live over there at the barracks, don't you?'

'The manager traded me out,' he says. 'For a boiling chicken.' He laughs. 'But I'm glad. I'd much rather be in the garden than in the factory. And Mr. Steffens is kind.'

'Him?' I ask.

'Yes, very kind,' he says. 'He talks with me as though I were a person. Just as you do.'

He bends down, pulls carrots out of the ground, picks a couple of asters as well, and gives me the bouquet.

'My name is Jan,' he says. 'And yours?'

'Regine Martens,' I say.

'Regine?' He thinks a moment. 'Regina. There was a girl by that name in my home town. Regina has a nice sound.'

He looks at me with those clear eyes. Until I see nothing but his eyes, no more face, just his eyes.

We are standing by the greenhouses and the sun is shining; I hold a bouquet of carrots and asters and I can see the P on his overalls and say: 'Jan? Jan has a nice sound, too.'

That's how it began. That was our first conversation. I didn't care anymore that I was speaking to a Pole. That it was forbidden. That I wanted never to speak to a Pole.

'Will you come back?' he asked.

'In an hour,' I said. 'When Mr. Steffens is here.'

But I would have come back anyway. To Jan. Although I really don't know why to him of all people. He was so different from the boys I'd liked until then.

'A German boy must be tough as leather, hard as Krupp steel, fast as a greyhound.' That was one of the slogans they'd drummed into us.

My girlfriends and I had made jokes about it. But some of it stuck. Men, we thought, should be tall, athletic, with chiseled features. You had to be able to picture them in a submarine or in the cockpit of a fighter plane.

Jan was tall, but certainly not athletic. More what we called limp – with those drooping shoulders and hesitant movements. Everything about him, even his walk, had something cautious, groping about it, as though he were afraid of bumping into something. No, he didn't have the look of the Iron Cross about him, nothing at all of the hero. He looked more like someone who slinks off when there's shooting.

A weakling. Yes, he was that type. That's what we'd called men like him.

Jan laughed when he heard that, much later. If you can talk about much later – our time was so short.

'That's it,' he said. 'That's me. I'm scared of guns. It's good I didn't have to go to war.'

It was during the night, down at the flooded gravel pit, behind the old brickworks. We went out there just once. I wanted to so much. To sit outside rather than in the shed, with the water gleaming, the frogs croaking . . . But I was wrong. The summer was over. The frogs had long since stopped croaking, and in the darkness the water was straight black.

'It's good I didn't have to go to war,' Jan said; and I asked: 'And the letter *P* on your overalls? Do you prefer that?'

He nodded.

'The *P* isn't a bullet. It takes away my rights, but it won't kill me. When the war's over, I can go back to living.'

He laughed again. 'I'm a real coward.'

Coward. With all he risked? Poles who had affairs with German girls wound up in a concentration camp, or they were hanged without trial, simply hanged. Jan knew that.

All the Poles knew it. And yet he continued to see me.

'We're standing up here on a tightrope,' he once said. 'Without a net.'

The end could come any night.

'No, Jan, you're not a coward,' I said.

'Nor you, *moje kochanie*.' He kissed me. 'It's just that we're scared.'

He kissed me, he was near me, and for the moment nothing else mattered.

Chapter Four

MORNING to night the attic. Nothing but the white walls, the dark-stained bed frame, the checkered bed covers, the stove by the door, the table with the flowered tablecloth, red roses, blue roses. I know it all by heart, every crack in the wall, every joint in the brown painted floorboards, even the smells that drift up to me. Potatoes fried with bacon. Pea soup. Crumb cake. And the days never end. I'd like to yank open the window, lean out, and scream.

'Just don't have hysterics,' Gertrud says. 'Better do something.'

But I finish the work she brings me much too quickly. Ironing, laundry to be mended, socks to be darned – there aren't enough socks at Henninghof for the time I have. Besides, I don't like to darn socks.

The worst of it is that I can't put on a light. About four twilight sets in, and I can't even read. Though it hardly matters, I have so little to read. Sometimes, when Gertrud bicycles to one of the neighboring villages on a Sunday, she comes back with books. The farmers don't have much. I guess by now I know everything that's available in the area, including several issues of *The German Farmer's Almanac*.

Recently, Gertrud even brought back Schiller's plays; they'd been lying in Haake's loft since the last war when people from the city had traded all sorts of things for eggs and potatoes, just as they do now.

Schiller's plays in red leather with gilt edges. Since then I've been memorizing *Don Carlos*.

Gertrud grinned when she brought me up the volumes.

'At least five pounds' worth,' she said. 'I hope it'll last you a while. Old Haake must have thought I was crazy when I said I wanted to take them, too. "What for?" he asked, and I told him I couldn't sleep and that's why I needed the books. "Naw, Trudi," he said. "What you need is a man, or at least honest work. It's good spring's almost here, and we'll start in again in the fields. You'll see, things'll go better then."'

She laughs and pounds the table.

'Old Haake's right, there. Come spring the war will be over, and we won't need books anymore, right, child?'

When Gertrud laughs, the room shakes, and you have to laugh, too, even if you'd rather cry. It's as though she were laughing with her whole body.

She has broad hips and thick arms and works like a man. In the summer she gets sunburned, and her blond hair bleaches out. It looks almost white then. But it darkens again in winter, and her red face pales and becomes tender. In winter Gertrud is pretty. But it doesn't last long, at most till April. She doesn't care. 'The main thing is the work gets done,' she says. 'And in any case I've already got one.'

By that she means her husband, whom she married five years ago. He's been on leave six times since then.

She doesn't speak of him often. 'If he comes back, I'll have him for long enough,' she says; and sometimes his letters are still sitting unopened in her apron pocket when she brings me my breakfast the following morning. Nights she beds down with Maurice, and treats him as though he were a husband. I guess he's become something like the farmer for her. They work together, he gets the biggest pieces of meat, and when she's mad, she yells: 'You idiot!'

Maurice likes her, too.

'She's like a cow,' he once said to me. 'A warm, gentle cow. But you musn't tell her that. She wouldn't understand it's a compliment.' Once in a while, when he brings up wood, he spends some time with me. We speak French together. Only then, though, because of the others.

Maurice had already studied German before the war. Now he makes almost no mistakes.

'I owe this course to your *Führer*,' he says. 'I really ought to pay him something for it.'

He's thirty-six, only four years younger than my father, and has a wife and ten-year-old son in Lyon. He carries their pictures in his breast pocket. 'I think of them constantly,' he told me once. 'But I'm a man. It's tough, *ma petite*.'

Gertrud thinks it's only natural.

'When the war's over, he'll hurry home,' she says. 'And he belongs there. He's working like a farmer now. But he isn't a farmer; he's a teacher. My husband's a farmer, he fits in here.'

Those are the conversations we sometimes have at twilight, when she sits with me in my room. We talk about Maurice and Jan and what will happen to her and to me. But it doesn't happen often. She has to gather wood and manure the fields with Maurice, has to thresh crops with him and fix carts and fences, reroof the barn, tend the livestock. It isn't true that there's no work during the winter. There's much too much for two people. I wish I could help them instead of memorizing *Don Carlos*.

'When the war's over!' Gertrud says. 'But then you'll be at the university and won't even notice us farmers anymore.'

Chapter Five

Today is Sunday.

Sundays everyone sleeps later on the farm. Sundays we have pastry for breakfast. Sundays the farmer's wife goes to church in the neighboring village.

It's almost two kilometers away. I watch her as she goes. She is big and wide. She walks very slowly, because of the pain in her hips. From the back, she looks like a big black rock pushing itself down the road.

When she meets someone, she only nods and walks on. She doesn't talk to people anymore since the death of her last son.

Visitors came this afternoon. Gertrud has heated the parlor to serve coffee. The farmer's wife stays at the large table next to the kitchen, the place where she always sits.

I open the door a crack, listen, hear voices and laughter downstairs. I think of my mother, remember how she sits at home in a chair and knits. Or unravels old pullovers, winds the yarn around a board, wets it, dries it, so that she can use the wool again. I see her movements, the way she bends her head, raises it, turns to me. I'd like to go to her, to take her hand, tell her I'm still alive, and to see that she's still there, as she has always been, because she is after all my mother, even if we have grown apart in recent times.

I don't think she even noticed it. She was much too busy with thoughts of my father and the daily hunt for food. Here an acquaintance who has windfalls in her garden, there a butcher who will sell you sausage broth even without a ration card, a farmer who has skim milk now and then. Sometimes we got a couple of empty tin cans from the cannery that we could use: tin cans in exchange for sugar beets, some of the beets for the loan of a syrup press, beet syrup for cigarettes, cigarettes for meat. My mother was on the go all day for barter.

As for me, it was off to school. No letup. Even as the front approached, what mattered for us was the diploma.

'Each does duty where he stands,' Dr. Mühlhoff said. 'And for the moment you stand here, ladies. After all, you've set your professional sights above head maid.'

He was referring to the harvest volunteer work, because of which summer vacation had lasted from mid-June to the first of September. Now we had to make it all up, even if we had hospital duty in the afternoon or if we had to serve tea at the train station to troops passing through.

'Hospital?' Dr. Mühlhoff said. 'Station? Send your mother. Get your diploma, become a doctor or, for all I care, chief inspector of the railroads. You'll serve Germany better that way.'

He was pretty stern, had been even before, when we'd had him as a teacher in a lower grade. Then he went to the front, came back three years later minus his right arm, and became our teacher again. He taught German and English. We found he'd gotten worse. He may have saved my life, though.

He was the first.

The second was an old prison guard with bushy white eyebrows. I don't even know his name.

Dr. Mühlhoff, in his mid-thirties, at least six feet tall, dark hair, dark eyes, a perpetual tan no one could explain.

'He looks great,' my friend Doris Weisskopf would say. 'Too bad it's Mühlhoff, the monster.'

The fifth of October. We're writing an in-class essay.

We have a choice of three topics:

1) Description of a picture: *The Crucifixion Group* by Matthias Grünewald.

2) A quotation from Goethe: 'Earn what you've inherited from your fathers, in order that you may claim it.'

3) A letter to a friend overseas on the meaning of the present war.

I took the third topic.

Even if it had been the eleventh of September, the time before Jan, I would have chosen that topic. A letter to a foreigner. A letter like a Goebbels speech. For at least ten pages I would have gone on explaining why Germany has to wage war. For its own good. For the good of all people and nations. To counter Bolshevism and world Judaism.

But it wasn't the eleventh of September. It was the fifth of October. Twenty-three days after Jan.

Naturally, to pick that topic was insane. Now I know it – because I have felt what it's like when they come and get you, shove you in a car, take you to a cell, lock the door. That topic! I knew I had to be careful, but I chose it and wrote.

'You wanted to bear witness,' said Jan. 'Like the martyrs. That happens. Sometimes you can't do otherwise.'

'You're awfully young, *ma petite*,' said Maurice.

'How stupid can you get?' said Gertrud. 'Even I wouldn't do that. And I only went to the village school. Some people get dumber and dumber by learning.'

A letter to a foreigner on the meaning of the present war. I wrote a letter about its senselessness. About the senselessness of all wars. The insanity of killing and dying. And about the importance of life. About friendship among peoples and nations. About peace.

I wrote and wrote and turned in my essay and was pleased and relieved. As though I'd done it for Jan. Gertrud is right about my 'stupidity.' But Gertrud isn't like me. Nothing bothers her. She's been able to love her Maurice very calmly, two years running now, as though there were nothing to it.

On the evening after we had written the essay, there was an air alert. I sat in the basement with Feldmann's son next to me again. And suddenly, in the space of a second, I realized what I had done. What it meant.

I went sick with fear. What did they call what I was doing in my essay? Sapping morale? Propagandizing for the enemy? And what was the punishment? Jail? Concentration camp? By then I was listening to Radio London and knew how enemies of the state were being treated.

The next day I hardly dared to go to school. I walked so slowly I got there late.

But Dr. Mühlhoff behaved as usual. We did English that morning. He had me translate half a page and said: 'Very good, Regine. Keep up the good work.'

I thought, he hasn't read it yet.

At the end of the hour, as I passed by him, Dr. Mühlhoff stopped me.

'Could you spare a moment, Regine?' he said. He

waited until the others had left the class. Then he stood up. He towered over me. I was sweating. My hands were cold and damp.

'I have something of a problem,' said Dr. Mühlhoff. 'Yesterday I looked through the essays quickly, and now I can't seem to find yours.'

He paused, picked up a pencil from the desk, put it back down.

'Your essay must have slipped in among my newspapers,' he said. 'And it probably wound up in the stove with them. What do we do now?'

I stared at him. I still didn't understand.

'What do you say?' he asked. 'Could you rewrite the essay? Obviously, you don't have to. Only you could spare me some difficulties. The Ministry might require to see the essays, and if one were missing . . .'

His face was expressionless. He was waiting.

'Yes,' I said.

'I don't remember anymore which topic you chose,' he continued. 'Wasn't it the description of the picture? That seems particularly suited to you.'

I nodded.

'Very good,' he said. 'Then I propose we both stay here at lunchtime, and you'll write your essay over. I'll see if I can get us something to eat. After all, it is my fault.'

He smiled. 'As you can see, we all have bad luck once in a while. As long as it can be corrected, though . . .'

I nodded again. So far I hadn't got a word out except yes.

'I find you've changed, Regine,' he said. 'Your father has been reported missing, hasn't he? In Russia? Yes, the war has demanded sacrifices of all of us.'

I was still.

'But the final victory is near,' he said, and he meant not a final victory, but an end. He sent out signals and assumed that I was among those who knew the code and understood.

'Then we'll have more time,' he said, 'and I'm sure we'll have a chance to talk peacefully.' He stuck a cigarette in his mouth, pressed the matchbox under his stump of an arm, lit a cigarette, nodded to me, and left.

'See you later,' he said.

That night I told Jan about it, and he made that comment about 'bearing witness.'

'You've accomplished one thing,' he said. 'Mühlhoff knows how you think. There's two of you now, and that can be useful. You have to watch yourself, though, watch yourself much more closely. We don't want to become martyrs, *moje kochanie*.'

Moje kochanie . . .

I hear his voice.

'*Moje kochanie*,' he says. It was so nice to hear him say that.

Has *he* become a martyr?

Chapter Six

IT all happened so fast with Jan and me. That night, the air raid: the next day, those few short words by the greenhouses . . .

'Why not?' Gertrud said.. 'It happens!'

We talked about it last night. The farmer's wife had already gone to bed. Gertrud, Maurice, and I were sitting at the big table drinking gooseberry wine. Sunday nights we stay up later than usual.

'But me of all people,' I said. 'I don't understand it. I'm not that way.'

'Nonsense, *ma petite*,' said Maurice. 'Of course you're that way. If it has to be, you're that way.'

'Love at first sight,' said Gertrud. 'There is such a thing. It's never happened to me. I guess I'm too slow, like a cow.'

Maurice and I burst out laughing, and she asked: 'What are you laughing at? It's not that funny.'

'No,' said Maurice. 'A cow is a beautiful thing,

38

chérie. And you probably never had to hurry like the little one.'

Gertrud got angry.

'What do you mean!' she pitched into him. 'You make it sound like she was in heat.'

Maurice put his arm around her and gave her a kiss on the nose.

'Now be quiet a bit,' he said, and kissed her ear as well. Gertrud blushed, as she always does when Maurice is tender with her.

'The things he does,' she said to me recently. 'When I think of my man, that bull in a china shop. Well, a person has to experience everything.'

'Now you be quiet,' Maurice said. 'I want to talk with the little one. Listen, *ma petite,* there's a German author by the name of Thomas Mann. He writes novels. Do you know him?'

I shook my head.

'Of course not,' Maurice said. 'Your *Führer* has banned him. He lives in America now, and when the war is over, you'll read his books. He has thought a lot about time, how fast or slowly it goes, depending. In one of his books, the *Joseph* novel – it's four volumes – he tells about old Jacob, who lived to be more than a hundred and who did everything in life at an easy pace, never hurrying. And then Thomas Mann talks about haste and leisure, roughly like this: The soul knows how much time it has for something, and sets its pace accordingly. And if it knows it has very little time left – then it has to hurry . . .'

'What does very little time mean here?' I broke in. 'Until when? Until death?'

I saw Maurice start. 'No,' he said. 'Of course not. I mean, for a specific thing. Sometimes, too, of course, for living.'

'Garbage!' Gertrud said angrily. 'Regine is still alive, you idiot,' and I said: 'Jan – maybe he's dead – maybe that's why he was in such a hurry. Not me but him.'

I put my head down on the table and cried.

'Now, *ma petite,*' said Maurice, and Gertrud started scolding.

'Now you've done it! Souls and time and death – what garbage. That's what comes of all those books, that's what you get.'

She put her arm around me and raised my head. With the corner of the checkered tablecloth she wiped my face, as though she were rubbing a calf dry. That occurred to me, even though I was sobbing. 'Calm down, Regine,' she murmured. 'He's still alive, your Jan. The war won't last much longer, then he'll come back, your Jan, he'll come back for sure.'

After that we sat together for a while longer. No one said very much.

No time. Jan had said it, too.

'We may have very little time, Regina . . .'

On the twelfth of September, my birthday, as I

entered the garden for a second time, he and Steffens were standing by the shed. Steffens was holding up a sack into which Jan was shoveling onions.

'Hi, 'Gina,' said Steffens. 'So there you are. Jan told me you'd been by.'

He threw a couple of onions into my basket.

'A pretty girl, isn't she, Jan?' he said.

Jan smiled at me and nodded.

'So what would you like?' asked Steffens.

'Whatever you can give me,' I said. 'Beets. Or carrots. And white cabbage.'

Steffens laughed.

'Did you hear that, Jan? As though she were the only one who wanted something. I have to deliver it all. They've already counted every head of cabbage.'

'Still, maybe there will be one left over,' I said. 'You see, it's my birthday.'

'You don't say!' Steffens exclaimed and dropped the sack. ''Gina's birthday! How old are you?'

'Seventeen,' I said.

'Seventeen!' He acted as though no one had ever turned seventeen before. 'Seventeen, Jan. And how old are you?'

'Twenty-two,' said Jan.

'So you could have gone dancing together today, if these weren't such crazy times,' said Steffens. 'Oh well, it may come sooner than we think. A schnapps, though, that we can have now.'

He opened the door to the shed. As I passed him,

he pinched my cheek. 'Seventeen!' he said, and he seemed much less horrible than before.

The shed was divided into two parts. In front there were crates of apples and pears, carrots, cabbage, beets, onions. In back there was a small room with a table, a couple of chairs, a sort of writing desk, and an old leather sofa.

'This is where I sleep when I don't want to see my wife,' said Steffens, and winked. 'So, where's the schnapps?' He got a bottle and glasses out of the desk drawer and poured.

'Cherry brandy. Kid stuff,' he said. '*Prost!* And now you get a birthday kiss.'

He took my head in his hands, and I put up with it.

'That's good,' he said. 'Even an old ass like me needs fodder. And now you, Jan.'

He pushed me toward Jan.

'No, Mr. Steffens,' I said, and pulled free.

'She doesn't want to,' he said. 'Why not? He's a nice boy.'

I wouldn't look at Jan.

'You shouldn't be like that, girl,' said Steffens. 'They're all people. Take my son, who's missing. Maybe he's sitting in a Russian prison camp. Maybe someone will be nice to him sometime.'

'But she is nice, Mr. Steffens,' said Jan, and Steffens slapped him on the shoulder and shouted: 'When the war's over, you'll go dancing together. *Prost!*'

He was a little tipsy. He was that way a lot.

He poured another round, and I had the feeling none of this was real. You've got to go, I thought. You can't stay here. A Pole. Steffens is crazy . . .

But I stayed. We sat at the table, and Steffens said: 'Now this is cozy,' and talked on about his son.

'He's the same age as Jan. Looks like him, too. When Jan came, I thought, that's him. But my Günther is in the hands of the Russians. He said he wouldn't let himself get caught by them, the ass, not by the Russians. He'd shoot himself first . . .'

'My father, too,' I said. 'He said that, too.'

Steffens gave the brandy bottle a shove. If Jan hadn't caught it, it would have fallen over.

'Your father?' he said. 'I know him. I knew him when he was unemployed and half-starved. He put on a good ten kilos later. No one who likes to eat that much shoots himself. My Günther neither. He likes women too much.'

'But the Russians. What they do to them,' I said. 'They're . . .'

'No, don't say that, Regina,' Jan broke in. 'There are good Russians, bad Russians, good Poles, bad Poles . . .'

'Good Germans, bad Germans,' Steffens added. 'And when the war is over, we'll send them all to hell, the . . .'

He slapped a hand over his mouth.

'I'm soused,' he mumbled. 'They'll have my head

if I go on this way. Just don't blow the whistle on me, 'Gina.'

He patted my cheek, stood up, went out. He'd drunk one glass after another. The bottle was almost empty.

'He's worried about his son,' said Jan. 'Sometimes when he drinks, he manages to forget.'

I stood up, too.

'Wait, Regina,' said Jan. 'I haven't wished you a happy birthday yet.'

He walked around the table and came up to me.

'Best wishes,' he said and kissed me, so lightly, I barely felt it.

'But . . .' I said.

'Sssh!' He put a finger to my lips. 'Don't speak. Tonight at ten, okay? Here.'

I turned and ran out of the shed. My basket stood by the door, filled with cabbage, carrots, and beetroot. Steffens was nowhere to be seen.

'What kept you so long?' my mother asked when I got home.

'Steffens gave me a brandy,' I said. 'In honor of my birthday.'

'Did he try anything?' my mother asked.

I said no, and that he wasn't really that way and had spoken of nothing but his son.

She took the white cabbage out of the basket and stared at it. 'So this is your birthday,' she said.

44

'Brandy with Steffens! Come on, let's at least have a cup of coffee together.'

She had set the table in the living room. A case lay beside my plate. I opened it and saw the locket that my father had given her on their wedding.

'But, Mama, it's not right,' I said.

She had begun to cry again.

'Take it,' she said. 'From Papa and me.'

In the locket there were two portraits. My father and my mother. So young. As young as Jan and I.

I had invited my friends – Doris, Ille, Gisela. But none of them had time after the raid; they were all busy cleaning up either at home or at relatives'. Doris Weisskopf came by just to ask if we had any spare pasteboard for her broken windows.

'We'll make up your birthday,' she said. 'The cake will keep.'

The cake was the main thing. There had been less and less food recently. Sometimes the stores didn't even have enough to give you what your stamps allowed.

Nevertheless, my mother managed to bake cakes for holidays. Almond cakes with rolled oats instead of almonds, with syrup instead of sugar and lard. Fruit tarts made of nothing but flour, skim milk, and apples. My mother had a cookbook she used, called *For the German Housewife in Wartime*.

'For the German Housewife Who Has Nothing to

Swap,' my grandmother mocked, when she saw it lying around. But my mother wouldn't listen to her.

'Think of Franz,' she said. 'When we win the war we'll have two, three times more of everything, much more than we had before.' She never said 'after the war,' always 'when we win the war.' She got that from my father. The same as me. Even I used to say 'when we win the war.' When I still wanted us to win. Before Jan.

'Before Jan. After Jan,' Gertrud once said. 'How it sounds! Like before Christ, after Christ.'

'Exactly,' said Maurice. 'And that's how it is for her. A turning point, a new era.'

Chapter Seven

'WHEN we win the war,' I'd say, in the time before Jan; and Doris found it amusing.

'When we win the war! That sounds so pathetic.'

'If you believe it, you should say it. You even have to,' I'd say, and Doris would grin.

She was always a bit mocking, just like her father who has a dueling scar and works as a vet. Another one who didn't have to go to war, though he was the vet for the Steinbergen garrison and wore an officer's uniform on certain occasions.

'What's more, they don't have any horses now,' said Doris. 'Just a couple of dogs.'

On Doris's birthday there was always a real cake, because Dr. Weisskopf got flour, eggs, and lard from the farmers.

'They should be reported,' my mother complained. 'Those academics. They still think they're something better. They aren't true National Socialists, they're just pretending. They had it good before. They didn't have to struggle like us.'

Doris laughed when I told her that.

'Your mother and her complexes,' she said. 'My father's in the party. And treasurer of the NS Medical League. And a reserve officer. He's everything he has to be. There's no way he's not a National Socialist.'

'Well,' I said. 'That's reassuring!'

Then we both laughed. I didn't take her nonsense seriously.

At the time I had no ear for signals. Even when Doris once drew me over to the other side, I didn't realize it.

It was in June, just before I volunteered for the harvest. The incident with Miss Rosius.

Miss Rosius, an assistant schoolmistress, slim, elegant, not old yet but already white haired. She taught biology and chemistry. She was generous, always ready to help, and didn't fret over trivia. If something didn't please her, she got sharp. Her class never bored me. It was because of her I wanted to study chemistry.

That semester in biology we studied ethnology. We already knew Miss Rosius didn't like ethnology.

'In my opinion there are more interesting subjects,' she said by way of introduction. 'But it's on the teaching schedule. So, they say there are different races. Eastern, Western, Dinaric. Yes, and naturally the Nordic race. That, of course, is the heart of the whole menagerie.'

48

We laughed. But it was blasphemous, of course, as though a preacher in the pulpit were making fun of the Holy Ghost.

'She doesn't have to handle it quite that way,' I said to Doris.

Doris was still laughing.

'Menagerie! I like it,' she said.

'Menagerie – what exactly do you mean by that?' asked Ilse Mattfeld.

Miss Rosius looked at her and smiled.

'How nice, for once you've chosen to participate in the class,' she said.

Ilse Mattfeld had joined us at the beginning of the year. She came from Berlin and was living with relatives. Until now she'd drawn hardly any attention. She sat in her place with arms folded, never raised her hand, kept to herself even during recess.

Doris and I didn't like her.

'If you ask me, she's getting ready,' said Doris. 'Like a June bug before taking off. She'll pull something, just you wait.'

After that biology class Ilse Mattfeld stood up at the front of the room and asked: 'Haven't you ever noticed that Rosius doesn't say "*Heil* Hitler"?'

Ilse Mattfeld was right. Miss Rosius did raise her hand when she entered the room, but then turned it into a gesture of dismissal and murmured: 'Be seated.' It hadn't, in fact, ever struck us. We heard '*Heil* Hitler' so much and so often. No matter what you did or where you went, it was always '*Heil* Hitler.' You hardly noticed it anymore.

49

'It's terrible,' said Ilse Mattfeld, and I agreed with her.

'You're crazy,' Doris criticized me after the class. 'Rosius does it out of sheer absent-mindedness. She's too smart to do something like that deliberately.'

'I don't know . . .' I said.

'Maybe the name is too holy for her,' Doris suggested. 'Like: "You shall not take the name of your Lord in vain," or however it goes.'

'Sometimes you really talk nonsense,' I said. 'Just don't let Ilse Mattfeld hear you.'

It was during the long recess. We were standing in the school courtyard eating our snack. Doris had a sandwich with liverwurst – she called it patients' cold cuts – and gave me half.

'Better than NS rubberwurst, right?' she said.

'Well, I think we ought to warn her.'

'Who?' I asked. 'Rosius?'

'We like her, right?' said Doris. 'You want her to get into trouble? Out of plain absent-mindedness? And because of Mattfeld? We'll talk to her, and if she still says "Be seated" after that, it'll be her own fault.'

We went over in the afternoon. Miss Rosius lived near the post office, in an old half-timbered house. Her apartment was full of Biedermeier furniture.

'It's from my grandparents,' she said. 'Would you like a cup of tea?'

'No thanks,' said Doris. 'We haven't got much time.'

'What's wrong? Can I help you in any way?'

'No thanks,' Doris said again. 'We actually just wanted to give you some advice.'

'Oh?' Miss Rosius seemed surprised, and when she heard what was the matter, she said 'Oh' again. Nothing more.

'Well, I guess we'll be going,' said Doris.

Miss Rosius accompanied us to the door.

'Thank you for coming,' she said. 'That was very considerate. You're right, I shouldn't be so distracted.'

I had kept quiet the whole time.

When we reached the street, I looked around. I was afraid Ilse Mattfeld would see us.

For the first time I had crossed over to the other side. I didn't even notice the change. And I retreated immediately, went on believing what my parents believed, what we read in our books, what we sang, heard on the radio, saw in the newspapers, what they preached to us at the German Girls' League.

The Jews are our misfortune.

Germans are better than everyone else.

The *Führer* knows everything.

The *Führer* will lead us to victory.

You mean nothing, your people mean everything.

One people, one empire, one leader.

I see us in our Girls' League uniforms, navy-blue skirt, white blouse, black scarf, standing in a circle around the flag, our arms raised in the Hitler salute.

'Our flag flies on before us,' we sing.
'Our flag is the new era.
And our flag will lead us on forever,
yes, our flag means more to us than death.'

'Did you really believe that?' asks Maurice.

'Yes,' I say. 'And it made me happy. I liked to join in, to belong. When we stood by the flag and sang, it was almost like church for me. Solemn. Truly holy. Those songs: "For freedom alone we'll give our lives, loose the flags on the wind. . . ."'

'My God, my God,' Gertrud moans.

'The campfire at night . . . Belonging to a community . . .'

'Stop it,' says Gertrud.

'But that's how it was,' I say. 'For me anyway. Maybe I needed something to believe in. I didn't know what lay behind it.'

'Such a pretty red apple,' says Gertrud. 'And so rotten inside.'

'Be glad you've left it all behind you,' says Maurice. 'You were as blind as a kitten, but now you can see.'

'But my parents weren't kittens. And they were still blind.'

'If your father was lucky and wound up a prisoner, he'll have opened his eyes,' says Gertrud. 'Most people only close their eyes as long as it serves their purposes.'

It served my parents' purposes.

'Good thing the *Führer* came along,' ran a line of my mother's. 'Or we'd probably have starved.'

But is that a reason to be so blind?

Once the words 'concentration camp' came up in our conversation.

'Of course,' my mother said. 'The Jews and the Communists are sent there to learn to work. They need that.'

She believed it. She didn't know any better. She didn't listen to foreign broadcasts, she didn't read much, she didn't know anyone who could tell her the truth. Still, to know that people are being thrown in a camp – isn't that enough? To know it and approve of it? . . .

Would she perhaps have approved of other things as well?

'Be quiet,' she scolded me when I tried to talk to her about it. 'The *Führer* knows what he's doing.'

'You mustn't condemn her,' Jan says. 'Soon everyone will know the truth. Then you must help her.'

We're lying on the sofa in the shed. In the dark. I can't see him. I can only feel him, his skin, his hair, the mole on his shoulder.

'Don't condemn,' he says.

In 1939, shortly after the invasion of Poland, ss people killed his father. He was a professor of geology at the university in Cracow. They took him from his apartment, along with other professors, with lawyers, doctors, merchants, engineers. Some were dragged off, thrown in concentration camps. Many were shot.

'They lay at the edge of the forest,' Jan says. 'I didn't understand at the time why my father was among them. He had never been involved in politics, he'd only written scientific books. He was among the best-known scholars in Poland. Later I understood that was the reason. Our intelligentsia was supposed to be wiped out.'

'Not condemn?' I say. 'But my parents are also responsible. We're all guilty together.'

'What do you mean by guilt?' Jan says. 'Poles also killed Germans. Hate for hatred and then more hatred. Someone has to put an end to it. Do you know the story of the Pied Piper?'

'Yes. But my parents weren't children anymore.'

'Many people never grow up. They run after anyone who will make them promises.'

I touch him.

'You should become a preacher.'

'Maybe,' he says. 'But not a Catholic preacher, because then I couldn't love Regina anymore.'

That was during our last week, just before the end. Is he still alive? Can he still forgive? I miss him so much.

I close my eyes. I hear his steps. Here he comes. We'll go away together. We'll begin everything over again.

Chapter Eight

GERTRUD was in town and ran into my mother. Near the train station. My mother wanted to slip by her, but Gertrud stopped her and said: 'You're Regine's mother. You visited her once at our place during the summer. How are things?'

My mother began crying and whispered: 'Don't you know what happened to Regine?' Then she told her all about the Pole who seduced me and how I fell for him without knowing what I was doing.

'But not a nasty word about you,' said Gertrud. Just "poor child, poor child," over and over.'

My mother thinks I died in the big air raid, as does everyone else in the city.

'It was probably the best thing for Regine,' she said, crying harder and harder. 'When I think of what they would have done to the poor child.'

I feel so sorry for her. First, my father. Then me.

But even she mustn't know I'm alive.

I think about my parents. My father, my mother, both born in 1905, grew up in the last war as I have in this one. My mother's father was a cabinet maker, my father's father a coachman. They lived on the same street and played together as children.

'I never had another man,' my mother said, whenever she talked about earlier times. 'He was the only one.' They had to marry in 1927 because of me.

'The truth is, we were much too young,' my mother said. 'So little money. The small change Papa made – it was barely enough for food and a roof over our heads.'

At that time my father was the bookkeeper in a hardware store. He was out of work in 1929, right at the beginning of the Great Depression. They had nothing left. They moved into a tiny room with a window on the stairwell. My father tried everything, but there was no work, not for my mother either.

'At first I cleaned other people's homes,' she said. 'But soon there were no more jobs. No one had any money.'

She told me those stories over and over again.

'Mama, tell me how it was before,' I begged, and then she would begin, almost always in the same words. About the welfare support that always lasted just three days, and how they had only one herring left to eat and my father threw it against the wall in desperation. 'Finally we couldn't even pay for that miserable hole of an apartment and had to move back to our parents'. I to mine, he to his. And you were still so little . . . that lasted over three years . . . I wouldn't wish it on anyone.'

I still remember it. We slept on my grandparents' sofa, I with my head by my mother's feet. During the day I had to sit still, because my grandmother fretted so over her furniture.

I can still hear her voice: 'A scratch in the cabinet!' She kneels on the ground, a cloth with polish in her hand; her gray bun rides up and down, and I won't get an apple because I scratched the cabinet. I fear my grandmother. Sometimes, when my father is around, I have to sleep in her bed. That's why I don't want my father to come.

My father lived just a couple of houses farther down. We never visited him, though, because his mother wouldn't let us in.

'She didn't want him to marry me,' my mother said. 'It was supposed to be a girl with money. But he chose me, and then he had to crawl back to the old woman for shelter. I guess if you hadn't been around, he would have hanged himself. He was that far gone. Thin as a rail, no more strength in his bones, no hope. Luckily, though, the *Führer* came.'

I've heard it so often I know it by heart.

'Then the *Führer* came, and Papa became a brown shirt, in 1930; there aren't many who joined the party that early. Richard Bösenberg took him along, and Papa said that same evening: "He'll do something for us, Hitler, he'll get us out of this mess, make life worth living again for us Germans." And Papa was right about that. It was bad until 1933. But then things got better.'

Every time my mother reached that point, she would look around the room. Her glance would travel from one piece of furniture to another until it reached the big picture of the *Führer* over the desk, and then she'd repeat: 'Yes, better. And only someone who lived through it can understand that.'

We got the apartment in 1933, right after Hitler came to power and my father became head clerk at the cannery. Dining room, study, bedroom, nursery, kitchen, bath. My grandfather made the furniture. He had promised my mother that from the beginning, and the wood had lain ready for some time. Buffet, sideboard, bookcase, everything dark and heavy, with carved doors.

'Old German,' my mother called it. 'Every piece is quality,' she says. 'Not factory junk like most people have.'

She was so proud of her apartment and her furniture.

'We owe it all to the *Führer*,' she said once when the sun was shining on her buffet.

Even my father found that amusing. It became a standard line with us. For example, if we had something good to eat, we'd raise our eyes to heaven and sigh: 'We owe it all to the *Führer!*'

But – and even though he joked about it – deep down my father believed it as much as she.

Me, too. With all my mother's stories in my head!

And things were going well for us. Head clerk –
that was something. And me in the upper school.

'But what about the war,' said Jan. 'When the war
began, didn't you see what a price you were pay-
ing?'

'I was just twelve years old. What did I know?
My parents said we'd had the war forced on us out
of envy, because Germany meant something again
in the world.'

'And when your father was called up? And when
the letter came, saying he was missing?'

Maurice asked me the same thing.

'My wife cried,' said Maurice. 'For three days.
She didn't want to let me go. Hide somewhere, she
said, let them fight this war by themselves.'

My mother cried, too. That's all I know.

'Maybe she doesn't want to admit she was
wrong,' Maurice has suggested. 'Neither to you nor
to herself.'

'But you've gotten older.' Jan wouldn't stop dig-
ging. 'You've learned to think.'

Learned to think? I learned mathematics and
French and English, sure. But not how to think.
Maybe Doris did better. Certainly at her house they
had conversations different from those in my home.
But only with the door and windows closed. And
people like Dr. Mühlhoff kept their real opinions
hidden.

'Surely not everyone!' said Jan, who couldn't understand it, because he'd grown up in another country. 'Think of the twentieth of July. For an attempt

like that, you need a large group of people. Not just a couple of loners.'

The attempt on Hitler's life. I know. All I heard from the people of Steinbergen were exclamations of joy at the *Führer*'s salvation.

Still, maybe they were only that way because we were that way. Maybe they were scared of us. I know others now, too – Dr. Mühlhoff, Gertrud, Steffens. Earlier they didn't allow themselves to be recognized for what they were.

'Sure,' said Gertrud. 'I'm not tired of living.'

'Of course I keep my mouth shut,' Steffens said, too. 'Careful, the enemy's listening in.'

From my birthday on we often sat together in the shed. In fact, whenever I went to get vegetables. Steffens knew what was happening with Jan and me. At the beginning he said nothing, but the way he looked at us, with that combination of good will and anxiety . . . yes, he knew it from the beginning. He didn't have any inhibitions around me anymore, swore at Hitler and everything connected with him – softly, so that nothing would go beyond the walls of the shed.

'I'm not tired of living,' he said, just like Gertrud. 'They know I'm an old Social Democrat. I got my beating right after the seizure of power. And how! That was enough. Your father was in on it, incidentally.'

'My father?' I asked. 'What do you mean, my father? He couldn't have been!'

'For sure,' said Steffens. 'He was a brown shirt.

The Nazis and the Reds went at it constantly. After thirty-three that ended; then only the Nazis could beat up on people. They had good hunting.'

'But not my father!' I exclaimed again.

'Don't get upset, 'Gina,' said Steffens. 'That was long ago. Your father wasn't the worst, and he has calmed down since. At the time he had a grudge against me, anyway. I caught him taking a chicken from my coop once. He couldn't forget that.'

My father, head clerk, who never went out without his hat, even to go from the house to the factory.

We're somebody, Regine, don't forget that.

Once he fired an assistant for a single stamp.

If you take a stamp, you'll take more. It always starts with small things.

Don't play with Schmieder's children, Regine. They're no company for you. Schmieder was a thief once.

Mind the words for honor, Regine. Honest, respectable, reverent, ambitious, contemptible.

'My father doesn't steal chickens!' I said.

'But that's the way it was,' said Steffens. 'He was hungry in those days. Your mother, too. And you. Sometimes it happens. Too bad, I should have given him the chicken. At least it would have put some strength in your bones. But I didn't have any idea what it was like. We always had enough to eat. And I already had a paunch.'

He patted my back.

'Let's drop it, 'Gina, that's old stuff. Your father grew a paunch of his own and we got along again.

61

They all got along with me again. He's got over his *Sozi** leanings, they thought. And it was true, at least superficially. That's why I'm sitting here in comfort.'

Steffens poured himself a glassful and downed it. He was drunk again.

'A couple of my comrades were different,' he said. 'They weren't pigs like me. Now they're in a concentration camp or long since buried. And your father, the old Nazi, is cooling his heels with the Russians, if he's still alive. Together with my Günther, maybe. It's all a blasted mess . . .'

That evening I wanted to ask my mother if it had really been that way. If my father had stolen chickens and beaten people up. But I didn't do it. When I got home, she was sitting at the desk on which Father's picture stood.

'Farmer Hille plans to slaughter a pig and needs tin cans for the sausage,' she said. 'For ten cans he'll give me a duck. But I've only got seven. Maybe I can round up three more.'

She reached for the picture and began crying. 'Roast duck! That was Papa's favorite dish.'

Whenever we had something special to eat she would talk about my father. I guess eating and drinking were the most important things to them.

'You're stuffing all your money down your throats,' my grandmother often scolded her.

*See translator's note.

'Never mind,' my mother would say. 'That's what Franz wants. We've starved long enough.'

She was proud of his paunch.

'He's gained ninety pounds in three years. I'd like to see someone else manage that!'

And then, when he became a soldier and returned half a year later on furlough, the paunch was gone. I hardly recognized my father. No more paunch, no more double chin, no more jowls or folds of fat.

'You look great!' I said. 'Really young. Like in your wedding picture.'

But my mother cried over the vanished paunch.

I pretend we're married, Jan and I. A room with light furniture, bookcases, a colorful carpet, van Gogh's sunflowers on the wall. We don't have any children; there's just the two of us. We're still at the university. Jan is studying law, and I perhaps chemistry. In the evenings we come home. We cook dinner. We eat. It's nice to eat together, but not as important as it was for my parents. Jan mustn't have a paunch. He should stay as he is, sit opposite me in the easy chair, his shoulders bent forward; should talk with me, think with me, love me in our apartment without fear. On the sofa in the shed I was always afraid.

Chapter Nine

'DON'T be afraid,' Jan said when I came to him the first evening, breathless because I had run so fast.

I had taken the path through the front garden. We lived on the ground floor; off the living room lay a small terrace with steps. My mother usually went to bed before me, shortly after nine, and heard nothing more. Only the sirens could wake her.

Jan is waiting in front of the shed. He pulls me in, shuts the door.

'I have to go right away,' I say.

'But you just got here,' he says.

'And if there's an alert?'

'Then you can run home fast. You were out walking. They can't forbid you to get some fresh air.'

'And you? You aren't allowed out in the evening.'

'I know where there's a hole in the wall.'

A small candle is burning in the shed. Jan has

covered the windows with sacking. It's cool. The bare floor, the shabby sofa – I want to leave.

'We're safe here,' Jan says.

'And Steffens?'

'Steffens means well.'

'You hardly know him.'

'It doesn't matter.' Jan smiles at me. 'I know.'

We had faced off like two strangers bargaining with each other, testing, matter of fact. But when Jan smiled, it suddenly got warmer, and everything changed. The candle threw a glow over the sacking, the sofa, the table. The shed looked like a haven. I didn't want to leave anymore.

Yes, that's how it was.

'Come.' Jan offers me a chair. He sits down on the other side of the table, opposite me, puts his arms on the table top, looks at me.

'You're so pretty in the candlelight,' he says. 'I knew a girl back home who looked like you.'

'Where is she?' I ask.

'I don't know. But you're here.'

He reaches a hand across the table and places it over mine.

'Thank you for coming.'

'I didn't want to,' I say. 'I still don't. I think it's terrible I'm here.'

'Because of this?' He points to the *P*.

I nod.

'It's forbidden,' I say. 'And it should be. We're at war. This kind of thing isn't allowed. It's wrong. Our soldiers . . . and my father, if he knew . . .'

I talk and talk and notice I don't believe it anymore.

'Be still, Regina,' says Jan. 'It's the war that's wrong, not that you're with me.'

He runs his index finger over the back of my hand.

'This is the first time I've talked with a German girl,' he says. 'And I've been here four years.'

'Four years?' I ask, and am shocked it's been such a long time.

'Four years,' he says. 'Four years ago they picked me up. I was coming out of the movies. I wasn't even allowed to say goodbye to my mother.'

'No!' I say.

'Yes, that's how it was,' he says. 'My mother has died since then.'

His finger is still running over my hand.

'Do you want to go now?'

I sit there and have no answer.

'If you want, we'll be sensible,' he says. 'You go home, and Steffens will send me back to the factory.'

'No,' I say.

He looks at me with his clear eyes.

'It's dangerous.'

'For you, too,' I say. 'Are you frightened?'

He nods.

'But I don't care.'

'Nor do I,' I say.

He draws my hand to him and lays it against his face. We stay like that for a while. I don't know how long.

'You must go,' he says. 'It's already after eleven.'
I stand up.
'Will you come again tomorrow?' he asks.
I nod.
He takes me to the door and strokes my face.
'Good night, *moje kochanie.*'
'What does that mean?'
'You'll find out tomorrow,' he says.

Sometimes I dream about Jan and me. He stands before me, holds out his hands, I feel him, I see his eyes, hear his voice.
But the dream almost always ends badly.

Chapter Ten

IT is February. I've been at Henninghof four
months now. The war goes on. The Americans and
the British are driving deeper into Germany. The
Russians have encircled Breslau. Over the radio
come rallying calls and reports of the atrocities com-
mitted by the Bolsheviks.

It started snowing again yesterday, heavy flakes
almost as big as pennies. They swirl in circles outside my window. The street is more deserted than
ever. Only a company of home guards comes by in
the morning and at noon – old men from Gutwegen
and the area, men no longer fit for service, who are
'supposed to defend the homeland with their rheumatism,' as Gertrud puts it. They have a few boys
with them, fifteen and sixteen year olds. They have
no uniforms, just armbands and a couple of rifles.
They're supposed to get bazookas eventually. They
pass, most of them morose and silent, and the street
is empty again.

I remember winter of last year. The fir and beech boughs in the Steinbergen city park bend beneath their weight of snow. There are seven of us: Doris, Ille, Gisela, me, Hotte Berg, and the two Jochens. Jochen Schmidt and Jochen Creutzer. Only Rolli Voss is missing; otherwise our dancing class would be complete.

Dancing lessons. Did I really ever take dancing lessons? The Creutzers' dining room, the table pushed to one side, the carpet rolled up. The dancing mistress's voice counts one, two, three, one, two, three, and Jochen Creutzer steps on my foot.

By then, official dancing lessons were no longer to be had. Jochen Creutzer's mother had organized a private class, though. She came to see my mother herself, in order to invite me to attend.

'The boys will be called up in the fall,' she said. 'So it would be nice to give them this treat.'

My mother was all aflutter. Mrs. Creutzer, wife of the chief physician at the Johanniter Hospital!

'Your good husband took out my gall bladder,' she said.

Your good husband! I was terribly embarrassed.

'Really?' said Mrs. Creutzer. 'Have you recovered? And Regine can come, can't she? Jochen would like that so much.'

She smiled at me, almost like a mother-in-law; and my mother nodded, although we had just received the news that my father was missing.

'I don't know if Papa would approve,' she said, when Mrs. Creutzer had gone. 'Still, maybe he'd want you to have some fun while you're young. And he has always thought a lot of Dr. Creutzer.'

The dancing lessons were held at the Creutzers' villa. Our four escorts wore suits instead of the Hitler Youth shorts they normally ran around in, and we found it hysterical when they practiced kissing our hands. We laughed so hard it never worked, which drove Mrs. Schwinge, the dancing mistress, to despair.

'Gentlemen!' she exclaimed. 'You'll never learn it that way!'

'How awful!' said Hotte Berg. 'We'll be leaving for the front soon and we still can't kiss a lady's hand properly.'

Mrs. Schwinge looked at him with round eyes. Her husband was also at the front.

Still, we managed to learn the fox-trot, the tango, and a slow waltz . . . even Jochen Creutzer.

I didn't really like him much. I was only flattered because he was so handsome and because everyone was after him. When he wanted to kiss me on the way home, I'd ward him off. Then he'd march silently along by my side. He'd try it again at my front door, and then I allowed it. It was part of the dancing lesson.

'My God, my God, what a fuss,' Gertrud said when I told her about it.

I look out at the falling snow and think how childish it all was.

That winter, though, when Hotte Berg and the two Jochens came back together on Christmas leave, it was no longer childish. Rolli Voss had already been killed, in his first battle and right on his eighteenth birthday.

The three others didn't mention him, but I had the feeling they thought about him constantly. They had changed, and not just because they now wore uniforms. They tobogganed with us down the hill in the city park, tossed us off the toboggan, stuck snowballs down our sweaters just like before. But their clowning had got sharper and harder, like the way they grabbed us.

Before their leave ended, Mrs. Creutzer threw a party. 'House ball,' she called it. My mother had made me a new dress specially, cut out of the bedroom curtains: white voile, close-fitting up top with a very full skirt and blue velvet trim around the neck and hem. The prettiest dress I'd ever had.

'You look charming, Regine,' said Mrs. Creutzer, and looked over at her son.

She had invited a lot of guests, including colleagues of her husband who, like him, were not required to do military service. There were flowers and candles on the table. A girl in a white cap served – soup and roast venison and stewed cherries, probably all gifts from patients. In 1943, things still weren't as tight as they got later.

'Just once let's pretend we're at peace,' said Mrs. Creutzer. Her husband looked at his son, who had to go back to Russia, and said: 'Peace?'

After dinner we danced. Jochen Creutzer danced only with me.

'I can't waste any time,' he said, when I suggested he ask Gisela, who had been Rolli's partner, to dance. 'Rolli would understand.'

We danced, and his mother followed us with her eyes the whole evening. She had the same look as the farmer's wife did later, when she saw me with her Walter.

But that evening at the Creutzers' I didn't understand yet what it meant.

Jochen drank a lot and quickly and talked and talked at me. For days before he had been quiet. Now he tripped over his tongue constantly, the words came out so fast. And it was all trivial, I can't remember any of it anymore.

As we stood a bit to the side between two dances, he with a glass in one hand, a bottle of wine in the other, his father joined us.

'Nice evening,' he said. 'We won't see anything like this again for a long time.'

Then he took the bottle from Jochen and said: 'Not tonight, my boy. Get drunk in Russia. It would be a shame to do it tonight.'

Jochen wanted to take the bottle back. But his father stroked his head with a quick, short movement, and Jochen let his hand fall. After that, he was much calmer. He said almost nothing more, even when we danced. I liked dancing without the talk. He had put his face against mine, I liked that, too.

The last dance was a slow waltz:

Give me once more in farewell both your hands, dear.
Good night, good night, good night.
Our story was sweet, it's come to an end, dear.
Good night, good night, good night . . .

Suddenly I saw that Jochen had tears in his eyes.

'Keep still!' he ordered me. And then he said:
'You have no idea what we're going back to. This
goddamned charade. Candles! Still, I guess they
mean well.'

We danced the number out, and the party was
over. On the way home, we crossed the park. He
kissed me there. I held still. I even liked it. But
when he began to fondle my breast, I pulled away.

'Regine,' he said. 'Stop it. Quit playing around.
You've done it long enough.'

'But I haven't been playing around!' I said.

He took me back in his arms.

'Come with me,' he said. 'Come back to the
house. No one will notice. Come on. I have to go
away again. We have so little time.'

I pushed him away. I said he must be crazy, what
did he think he was doing, and suddenly he started
screaming at me. He screamed that he was going to
the front to die, and if he had to die for us the least
I could do was sleep with him once before he died,
and what kind of fantasies did I have about my
stupid virginity, did I think it was more important
than his life.

He stood there and ranted. Finally he tried to

73

throw me in the snow. It was well after midnight and there was no one around. I screamed, but no one heard me.

Suddenly he let me go, turned away, and disappeared.

'He just left you standing there?' Doris asked the next day. 'And you had to go home by yourself? That whole long way? I don't believe it!'

'Now listen,' I said. 'That really wasn't the worst of the whole thing.'

I wanted to know if Hotte Berg had tried it with her, and she said no, but that she would have done it, for sure, and that she loved Hotte and nothing else mattered.

'But you don't even know if you'll ever get married!' I said, and realized only later what nonsense our mothers had beaten into us.

'You lose your virginity only once. It's the most precious thing you have. Save it for the right man.'

The right man. It sounds good. But the right man for our mothers was only the one they married.

Jochen Creutzer was the wrong one. That's why I didn't do it. But when I think of him I regret it. Walter Henning was also the wrong one. Still, I'm glad I did it.

Jan was the right one, and it didn't matter one bit whether he was the first or not.

Jochen Creutzer was killed six weeks after the

party. His mother came to our house to tell me. She laid her head on my shoulder and cried, and I had a bad conscience. About Jochen. And about her.

That's why it happened with Walter Henning. But it wasn't nice. I couldn't think about it for a long while. Every time I did, my mouth would go dry with disgust.

Never again, I thought. I don't want to ever again. It's repulsive. Never again.

Jan wiped away all of that.

Jan and I. It's dark. I run through the garden. He is standing by the door. He pulls me inside the shed. The candle is burning. This time he kisses me.

'Moje kochanie.'

Already on the second night.

'Moje kochanie. Moje kochanie.'

And I want it. I forget Walter Henning and Jochen Creutzer and my mother and the P and the fear. I want it and Jan wants it and everything is all right.

Moje kochanie. Moje kochanie.

His face goes vague in the candlelight. I can only see his eyes clearly.

'What does moje kochanie mean?'

'My love.'

Later I tell him about Walter Henning.

'You felt pity,' Jan says. 'Pity is good.'

'But you're not the first one.'

'All the same,' he says. 'Now I am.'

'I love you, Jan.'

I had never said it. To anyone.

I love you. It's a good thing to say.

That night there was another air alert. I was just about to leave when the sirens went off.

'You go first,' Jan said.

'And you?' I asked.

'Run!' he said. 'Quick!'

My mother was already standing in the hall with her suitcase when I got there.

'I went for a walk,' I said. 'I had a headache.'

'Are you crazy!' she scolded me. 'Now, when the alert comes so often!'

'Can't I get some air once in a while without your being upset?' I said, and thought for sure she would know by looking at me what had happened. But she believed me.

I grabbed my suitcase and ran after her.

Had Jan made it?

In the basement, the question spun through my head like a top. I was afraid, just as afraid as I had been during the air raid, but it was different. A crawling, boring, gnawing fear. I've had it ever since.

Why did I fall in love with Jan, Jan of all people?

'You always ask the same thing,' Gertrud says. 'That's just the way it is. Not just for you.'

'Because he was different,' Maurice says.

I think Maurice is right.

'You were like a kitten,' he told me once. 'Blind.'

I needed something to open my eyes. A person. An event. I had already been prepared by Jochen Creutzer's death, by the farmer's wife and her dead sons, by the dying that came closer and closer.

Germany must live, even if we have to die.

Our flag matters more than death.

Did those sayings make sense?

Death: that had always been just a word. Now the word became reality.

Did the sayings make sense?

I had begun to ask questions. I just hadn't realized it yet.

For example: Germany, a people without land.

But at the same time: Germany needs sons. German women, give your *Führer* sons.

Why? If there wasn't room for them, why all those sons? In order to conquer new land? So they could die conquering new land?

Contradictions I couldn't grasp.

'When a people is losing a war, you call the sons cannon fodder,' said Doris. 'But we're winning, so for us they're heroes.'

She made more and more remarks like that. Hotte Berg had been killed, too, the third in our dancing class.

Doris came to our house one evening, late; my mother was already in bed. She stood in the door-way, breathless, as though she had run the whole way, and said: 'Hotte is dead.'

Then she sat down and cried; and when I wanted to comfort her, she said: 'Do be still. What do you know? It's impossible to talk properly with you anyway.'

Will I ever see Doris again? Then we could finally do that – talk together.

Chapter Eleven

THE army communiqué of February 27 – we heard it yesterday evening. Another of the many they set before us day after day. Facts, phrases, truth, lies, all mixed up. An unending string of defeats twisted into victory:

> In central Pomerania, on the outskirts of Bublitz and Rummelsburg, independent units have engaged in heavy defensive combat against Soviet advances to the northwest . . . On the East Prussian and Samland front the Bolsheviks, reeling from their heavy losses, have only now fully resumed their attack to the northwest of Kreuzburg. Our divisions, in fierce combat for days now, have prevented a breakthrough . . . Following an extremely heavy advance artillery barrage, the Canadian First Army resumed its major offensive between Niederrhein and Maas . . .
>
> Our reserve troops have rushed into combat against the attackers and are maintaining a defensive front . . .

At Dünkirchen, our artillery smashed an attempted attack by enemy armor . . .

In Pomerania, units of the ss Yeomen's Grenadier Division *Wallonia* under ss Colonel Capelle fought with exemplary fortitude and fanatic determination.

'They'll win themselves to death,' says Maurice.

We've long since lost the war. Yet more and more people have to die on the front and in the bombed-out cities. Evacuees from Dresden have been housed with some of the farmers in the village. When Gertrud tells me what they report of the terrible raid, the bombs that fell on Steinbergen hardly matter. Over 200,000 people died in Dresden. Two hundred thousand. I say the words out loud to myself. I can still do it. I am one of those who are alive. But I've grown even more fearful since yesterday.

In the afternoon Gertrud came to my room with bread, a tin of meat, and a pot of tea. She pushed the chair over to my bed and put the tray on it, all very quietly.

'Thumert is here,' she whispered. 'He's sitting downstairs now with Mother and eating. He'll be going to his room soon. You mustn't move as long as he is here. Not a step! Lie down. Take a chamber pot to bed if you have to. He'll be off tomorrow, he just wants to pick up his guns.'

She stroked my head.

'There's nothing to worry about. He won't come up here. But be still. I have to hurry back down now. Bolt your door.'

She left. I heard her step and a man's voice in the stairwell.

Thumert. We hadn't expected him to show up again. He was the owner and editor-in-chief of the Steinbergen newspaper. He went hunting in Gutwegen. He'd had a room at Henninghof for over twelve years. In the time before Hitler he virtually belonged to the family. Later, once Thumert became a head Nazi, old Henning would gladly have thrown him out.

'Our Final Victor,' Doris had christened him, because his headlines almost always contained the phrase 'Our Final Victory.' At one time – before Jan – I had liked his articles. He put everything so clearly and simply that any doubt seemed absurd.

'At least it isn't all puffed up,' my mother, too, would praise him. 'Anyone can understand it. When you read it, you know why we have to keep on fighting.'

Later, I understood the danger in his writing.

'He twists facts until they turn somersaults,' said Steffens. 'A regular magician. I remember his paper from before. Thumert was true blue to the emperor then, and he would just as soon have brought back Kaiser Bill. But come thirty-three he was into the party in a flash. What he printed from then on in that rag of his – hard to believe it was the same man.'

81

Thumert, the famous Thumert! When I met him during the harvest, I thought he was wonderful. I had imagined him completely different, much older and more sober. He was forty-two, thin, cocky, and gay; and when he ran about the farm in his gym shorts, he looked like a young man.

The first time he saw me, he whistled through his teeth.

'Who've you got here?' he exclaimed. 'Why wasn't I told? I would have come sooner!'

The very first evening he led me outside to the bench in front of the house and talked with me. He told interesting stories, stories about the Tibet expedition in which he had participated because he was a journalist and a good mountain climber. But I wanted most to hear about his work – how you put together a paper, what the most important things are, what skills you need.

'You'll question me to death, girl,' he said. 'I'll tell you what: join us. Become a journalist. You can start out with me.'

'Don't go putting dumb ideas in her head, Mr. Thumert,' said Gertrud, who had set herself down beside us. 'They can all start out with you, we've heard that before.'

He laughed, and I said I wanted to study chemistry anyway.

'Watch out for Thumert,' Gertrud warned me the following morning. 'He's a real skirt chaser.'

'But he's more than twenty years older than I am!' I said.

That evening he tried, though. While I was down by the brook behind the house, fetching water for the wash, he crept up on me. I struggled, and when he wouldn't stop and blocked my way, I threw a bucket of water down his shirt.

He stood there, drenched from top to bottom. He looked so funny I laughed.

Thumert wasn't laughing.

'You damned little witch,' he spat, turned around, and disappeared.

At the time, Gertrud was delighted.

'It'll do him good!' she laughed, and slapped her leg. But when we spoke about it again up in my attic room several weeks ago, she said: 'He'll hold that against you. Vain as he is. There was someone here from his paper once, and she told me he drives out every woman who won't give in. Oh well, it's lucky they've called him up to Berlin, so he won't be coming here anymore. Only after our final victory, he wrote.'

I bolted my door and lay down. I was so afraid I hardly dared turn. Perhaps that's why I had such a terrible dream during the night.

I dreamt of Jan. We were in the shed. We lay on the sofa. He didn't move. I tried to speak to him, but he didn't answer. I wanted to get up and leave, but I couldn't move either. And suddenly a giant figure came at us, a giant black figure with a stone in its hand. It came closer and closer . . .

At some point I began to scream. I heard myself screaming, half woke up, jumped out of bed, ran screaming to the door, unbolted it . . . Only then did I come to. I was standing in the stairwell. The beam of a flashlight found me. Thumert.

He squinted and looked at me. Then he said: 'Well, what do you know! Regine the virgin!'

Downstairs a door slammed. Footsteps. Gertrud ran up the stairs.

'For God's sake!' she cried. 'Regine!'

I let myself fall on the top step. I was soaked in sweat and shaking so hard my teeth chattered.

'I thought you were dead.' said Thumert.

Gertrud ran into the room, fetched a blanket, and put it over my shoulders.

'Are you going to betray us?' she asked.

Thumert didn't answer.

'Mr. Thumert,' said Gertrud. 'My mother has lost four sons. That's enough.'

Thumert looked at me and said: 'Our darling, the Pole's girl.'

'Just a minute,' said Gertrud. 'Since you already know, let's talk frankly. Obviously you can go and denounce us. Then we'll be run off the farm and they may hang us, even Mother, and she probably couldn't care less. But I do. The war will be over soon, you know that as well as I – you're no fool. And what's more, you know we're going to lose.'

'I won't listen to any more of this,' said Thumert.

'Oh yes, you will,' said Gertrud. 'The rest is still

to come. The war will be over soon, and then others will get it for a change. People like you. So if you betray us now . . .'

'Shut your mouth, Trude,' Thumert shouted. But she went on talking.

'Someone is bound to survive, someone who will make the rounds and talk about what Thumert did here at the very end.'

She fell silent and looked at him. Thumert was quiet, too.

'So,' Gertrud said, 'you listen for a minute. If you keep your mouth shut, if you keep still – then I promise you we'll put in every possible good word for you. We'll even say it was you who brought Regine here. We'll say anything you want. Even that you were always opposed to Hitler. Whatever you want. As far as I'm concerned, you can have it in writing.'

She spoke faster than she had ever done before, with no commas or periods and without taking a breath.

Thumert began to laugh.

'That's incredible!' he said. 'An incredible deal. My little Trude, I admire you. You are an outstanding specimen of the German peasantry. Come on, give it to me in writing.'

We went downstairs, and Thumert dictated what I should write. That he found me on the night of the raid and brought me to Henninghof. And that I was deeply grateful to him for my rescue.

'Not Henninghof,' said Gertrud. 'Write "brought to safety," Regine. Who knows what may still happen to you, Mr. Thumert; then someone might find the note and the address. That's out of the question. We'll give it to you later . . .'

Thumert pocketed the note.

'You know the funniest part of all this?' he said. 'I wouldn't have betrayed you. The fact is, I liked your father, Trude. And I take off my hat to your mother. To you, too, for that matter. And as far as the child there goes – well, what sort of person am I? I wouldn't soil my hands.'

'Then you can give back the note,' Gertrud declared.

He shook his head.

'A gift is a gift. It might come in very handy, you said so yourself. Besides, I know for a fact you've got something going with Maurice. And I'm keeping that for myself, too. He may want revenge someday. Then we can visit him together in Lyon.'

He grinned, and Gertrud said: 'Someone ought to punch you in the mouth.'

The next day, before Thumert left, he came up to the attic to see me again.

'You needn't worry,' he said. ''You'll make it all right. Incidentally, short hair suits you. You look like Jeanne d'Arc. Are you sure you won't become a journalist? I doubt I could help you now. Still, who knows – we've survived so much already.'

86

Maurice turned white with rage when we spoke of Thumert that evening.

'If I'd been there,' he said, 'I would have throttled him.' He opened his balled fists, curled his fingers in the air.

'By God, throttled him. That pig! It's people like him who are to blame. They were smart enough and knew what they were doing. They have us on their conscience.'

He looked over at the pictures of Gertrud's brothers.

'Just watch, that pig will get away with it.'

It was a long time before he calmed down again.

Chapter Twelve

I don't know why the days are so endless. I stand at the window, and it's as though I hear time dripping slowly, very slowly.

Sometimes the farmer's wife comes to see me in the attic. Heavy and panting, she climbs up the stairs. She sits down on the chair and is silent.

She can only speak again after a while. She says: 'They went for wood today.' Or: 'Willy Kleinmann is back. He's lost his legs.' Or: 'It's going to snow again. I feel it in my bones.'

I say yes and no and really, and I wait. I know she has only come to ask her question.

'Was it nice for him the last day?' she asks finally.

'Yes,' I say. 'Very,' and that is enough. She wants no more. Just to hear again how her Walter had it good on that day. Afterward she sits on her chair and is silent. Sometimes I think that she's turning to stone. That at some point she will really become a black statue: a sorrowing mother.

In the parlor, which is used only on holidays, hangs her picture. The wedding picture. She looks very much like Gertrud in it, only she's slimmer and more delicate. A lock of hair tumbles across her forehead; she is laughing, and the man at her side looks proudly into the camera.

I only know old Henning from Gertrud's stories.

'He wasn't dumb, my father,' she says. 'He kept his farm in good order. And read the paper every day, even during the harvest. When Hitler came to power in thirty-three, he said there would be a war. But no one in the village listened to him; they were dazzled with their National Peasants' Cooperative and their National Food Estate and all that trash. They thought, now every cow will grow five udders. Well, now he's dead.'

Old Henning died shortly after his second son. Of pneumonia.

'It was really grief,' says Gertrud. 'Heinrich and Karl – he couldn't cope with it. Mother has had to live through four. But not much longer, either.'

She looks at the pictures of her brothers.

'Odd,' she says. 'I think it's odd. So much is forbidden. Swiping apples, for example. Or calling your neighbor a "stupid pig." For that you get punished. But shooting down four sons, that's permitted. On top of it, our Walter died through sheer oversight. The last one doesn't have to go, you know; he's spared because three is enough, even for the party. But in Walter's case, some ass messed

up because there were still people named Henning
left in the army. Now he's dead, and no one will be
punished for it.'

'That isn't just your *Führer*, though,' says Maurice. 'It can happen anywhere. *C'est la guerre, chérie*,
even if one doesn't understand it.'

Walter came home on leave while I was a harvest
volunteer at Henninghof. He came on the tenth of
August and had to leave on the twenty-fifth. The
last son. And the youngest. His mother's face went
soft when he was near her. She watched him constantly.

'Like a cow and her calf,' said Gertrud. 'Walter,
stay with mother.'

But he wouldn't do it. During the harvest, everyone who could still walk was in the fields. Besides,
he preferred to be with me.

'He runs after you like a dachshund,' said Gertrud. 'You know, there are plenty of girls in the
village who are just waiting for some guy to come
on leave. But nope, you have to be the one.'

She didn't like me then, during the summer. She
kept away and when she saw her brother was after
me, she tried to talk him out of it.

'Yeah, you with your snappy "*Heil* Hitler," 'she
says now. 'I was already worried you'd make trouble about Maurice. And then Walter on top of it.
"Don't burn your fingers on her," I said to him.

90

"She's a regular Girls' League bitch." But he wouldn't listen. Anyway, he didn't want to talk politics with you.'

Of course, she noticed what happened. Even before we talked about it later, up here in the attic, she knew.

'Sweet of you,' she says. 'Walter, he never got anything out of life anyway. The other three, at least they were men. But that one!'

Walter was nineteen. 'Cast in a different mold,' said Gertrud, 'A bookworm.' He had gone to the middle school at Steinbergen and wanted to make up the diploma later.

'Then I'll become a teacher,' he told me. 'In history and geography.'

That was two days after he arrived, during the noon break. We sat under the big linden tree and ate cherry soup with dumplings. It was a hot day; you perspired even in the shade. We had been gathering rye since six. The sharp beards had pricked my arms and legs. They had even lodged in my overalls. Everything itched and burned.

'Do you like history?' he asked.

'Not at the moment,' I said. And when I saw the disappointment in his face: 'We went through the Napoleonic Wars just before I came here.'

'I like the Middle Ages best,' he said. 'The Hohenstaufen, for example.'

'How would you like to keep going?' yelled Gertrud, who was already back in the field.

'Stay put,' he said. 'You aren't used to the work yet. I'm here now, anyway.'

I worked on, though, mainly because of Gertrud.

That evening I almost had sunstroke. My arms were red and swollen. After washing the dishes I wanted to lie down.

As I was drying my hands, Walter came into the kitchen.

'I'm going out for a bit,' he said.

'Go along, Regine,' said the farmer's wife. 'Walter, he enjoys it when he has a chance to talk with someone.'

'Come on, Mother,' Walter mumbled; and Gertrud said: 'You'd better stay here, there's a storm coming.'

'Not today,' said the farmer's wife. 'I feel it in my bones.'

She looked at me. Her face was pale and old under the black kerchief, with deep lines from nose to mouth and circles under her eyes.

'Go on,' she said.

I went walking with Walter, that evening and the evenings that followed, always the same way: along the village street and through the fields to the edge of the forest, where the uprooted beech lay. There we sat on the tree trunk and talked about all sorts of things – about history and about books and about our childhood experiences and how we imagined the future. The evenings were warm and still, with only the sounds of the forest or now and then the hum of enemy bombers as they flew overhead. We acted as though they were nothing but the chirping of crickets.

Once Walter started in about the war.

'It's hell,' he said. 'I'm afraid to go back out. I'd rather crawl into a hole somewhere. During the last assault, we had . . .'

He broke off, and said quickly: 'Now the Alps, I'd love to see those. Not just on the map, I know them that way . . .'

I liked listening to him. I talked easily with him, much better than I had earlier with Jochen Creutzer. He knew a great deal and had a lot of ideas of his own – that seemed to run in the family. To sit with him on the edge of the forest in the evenings after work – crickets chirped, frogs croaked by the stream, now and again a star fell – yes, it was pleasant. Only he couldn't come too close to me. It made me cringe. He was too pink for me – pink skin, reddish-blond hair, his eyebrows and eyelashes, too. And everything was so delicate, his hands, his feet.

Strangely enough, Jan resembled him, slender and not very sturdy, just like Walter, although he wasn't pink. With Jan it attracted me. I wanted to take hold of Jan, feel his skin, it was like a compulsion. With Walter, on the other hand, I found it unpleasant if he even just tickled me with a blade of grass.

'What's wrong?' he asked one evening. 'Am I so repulsive?'

'What do you mean?'

93

I pretended I didn't understand him.

'What do you mean? Why do you say that?'

'Oh well.' He let fall the hand he had stretched out to me. 'Usually . . . but let's forget it.'

'One doesn't have to right away . . .' I said.

'Right away?' He laughed. 'That's good, right away. I'll be here another eight days. Right away is a fairly relative notion.'

He reached out his hand again. 'Don't you see, Regine, I love you.'

Oh God, I thought, no.

'We have so little time,' he said, and I let him kiss me. I felt like I was being forced to eat June bugs. But Walter was happy. He virtually danced his way home.

So little time. I was hearing it for the second time already.

And later Jan said it.

All the men who wanted me had no time. And all three are dead.

I think that, and the thought goes through me like a needle.

Jan can't be dead. I have to find him again.

If Jan is dead, I don't want to go on living.

Naturally, everyone on the farm knew what was wrong with Walter.

'God oh God, the poor boy was head over heels in love!' Gertrud still shakes her head when she talks about it. 'He was ready to hug the pitchforks. Also, I saw you weren't head over heels in love. The bitch is being choosy, I thought. I could have killed you.'

I felt her attempts to drive Walter away from me at the time, as well as the silent battle she waged with her mother.

The farmer's wife wouldn't be distracted. She said nothing. But she watched me unswervingly, would turn away her head, look at me again. And in the evenings she would wash up herself so that we could go for a walk.

Two days before Walter's departure, as we were eating dinner, she said: 'You sleep late tomorrow morning, Walter. Don't go out to the fields.'

'The wheat has to come in,' said Walter.

'Regine will also sleep late,' said the farmer's wife. 'And then you can plan a nice day together.'

'And who's going to bring in the wheat?' asked Gertrud. 'Maurice and I, I suppose? Just the two of us? How?'

She was right. Two weren't enough. It took at least three people: one to fork the sheaves from the wagon and raise them up to another person in the hayloft, who took them and passed them on to the one who piled them in the barn.

The farmer's wife stared at her plate.

'The wheat can stay out for a while.'

No farmer says something like that without a reason, and everyone fell silent and accepted it.

The next morning I slept until eight. Walter was already downstairs when I came in. The farmer's wife had set the breakfast table for us. In the center of the table stood a plate of deep-fried pastry, yellow from all the eggs, topped thick with sugar, still warm and crisp. She sat down next to Walter and put one piece after another onto his plate, until he said: 'Enough now. Otherwise I'll have to stay here and go back to bed to digest.'

'Then go,' she said, and brought a bag out of the kitchen.

'There are sandwiches in there. And cake. And a flask of coffee. And you don't have to be back before evening.'

She accompanied us to the gate and watched us go.

Suddenly I heard her voice: 'Regine!'

I turned around. She gestured, and I came back again. She stood at the gate, black and old. Her eyes had a look I had never seen in them before.

'Be good to him,' she said softly.

I don't know if I was good to Walter Henning. I did try to be. I thought of Jochen Creutzer's death and of what he had said about dying and our virginity, and I thought of Walter's fear and of his brothers and of what awaited him at the front. But most of all I thought of the farmer's wife.

'Was it good for you?' asked Walter.

We lay out by the bog lake. The walk there had taken almost two hours, through the fields, later through the forest. Walter had talked about the South Pole. It was hot, and I said I wished I were an Eskimo, so he started in on the South Pole.

'So you'll feel a little cooler!' he said.

But I didn't really listen. I kept remembering the words of the farmer's wife, and whether I should do it, and that it would just have to be.

I don't even know if Walter wanted it. But I didn't struggle when he took me in his arms. He went further, and I still didn't struggle, and finally it happened.

'I love you so much, Regine,' he said. 'Do you love me, too?'

I nodded. It didn't really matter anymore. But when he asked 'Was it good for you?' I began crying. 'Don't be sad,' he said, and caressed me. 'I'll come back. I'll see to it I come back, and then it will get better and better. I'll get my diploma and go to the university, and we'll marry, and everything will be great. Don't cry.'

I closed my eyes. He was so pink. I shuddered. Never again, I thought. Never again.

When we got back to the house, the farmer's wife looked at me questioningly. I felt how I blushed, my face, throat, even my arms. Then she did what she had probably done very rarely in her life: she pulled me close and stroked my head.

Walter left the next day.

In September, we received the notice of his death.

> My last and dear son, my good brother, our brother-in-law, nephew, and uncle, Private First Class Walter Henning, has followed his three brothers in death. With deep sorrow: Frieda Henning, née Seifert, Gertrud Happke, née Henning, in the name of all his relations.

I met Jan shortly after that. From then on I could think about Walter again.

'Was he happy on the last day?' asks the farmer's wife, when she sits with me in the attic. I say yes, and she looks at me as though I were a part of Walter.

I think that's why she took me in when I knocked on her window in October. That's why she's hiding me up here.

Perhaps Walter Henning is among those who have saved my life.

But it was good for the first time with Jan.

Chapter Thirteen

JAN and I. I close my eyes, and the walls of the attic vanish, the bed, the chair, the window with the muslin curtains. Jan and I. His hands. Our voices in the half-light.

'Talk to me, Jan. What was it like for you, growing up? What was it like where you lived?'

'When I was eleven, we moved to Cracow. My father became a professor at that time. We had an apartment near the park. In an old house with stuccoed ceilings, bay windows, big rooms . . .'

'You had all those things in Poland?' I ask, and he laughs.

'Cracow! Do you think wolves run in the streets there? They called it the Polish Athens, Cracow. We have one of the oldest universities in Europe. And our marketplace – you should see our marketplace, the Rynek Glowny; it would take your breath away. And the Church of St. Mary's with the Veit Stoss Altar!'

'You had that?' I ask in amazement.

'Do you think everything beautiful belongs to the Germans?' he challenges me. 'The Veit Stoss Altar belongs to us; you took it away from us.'

'Not me.'

'I know. Let's not talk about it anymore.'

But we start it over and over again.

The war, the war.

'Why do we always talk about the war, Jan?'

'Because the war is our life. If it weren't for the war, I wouldn't be here. If it weren't for the war, we wouldn't be sitting in this shed. If it weren't for the war, my parents would still be alive. If it weren't for the war, your father would be at home. Everything we're doing, we're doing because of the war.'

'If it weren't for the war,' I say, 'I might have taken a trip to Cracow.'

'You would have sat in a café on the Rynek Glowny, and I would have come in and seen you. What a lovely girl, I would have thought. I'd have come up to your table. "Pardon me, may I join you?"'

'There's an empty table over there!'

'But you're sitting here.'

'Would you have done that?'

'Yes, *kochanie*. No matter where I met you . . .'

I close my eyes and dream. Jan and I. We stroll through the streets of Cracow. He shows me the market, the Church of St. Mary's, the drapers' halls.

We window-shop, we sit on a bench, he holds my hand, we kiss. All without fear.

Reality was the shed and fear.

Peak season at the cannery ended in late September. The Poles at the barracks were distributed to other places of work.

'You stay with me, Jan,' said Steffens. 'Here in the shed. Officially, you live with us next to the horse stable. Someone keeps swiping apples from me at night, though, so it's good to have someone in the garden. Just don't run off, boy. I'm responsible for you.'

No one had ever stolen any produce. He just wanted to help us.

'Damn it all,' he said. 'This war, and you so young. Who knows what lies ahead for you. Those damned pigs, they're cheating you out of your youth.'

He brought blankets for the sofa and set up a small stove. Though the fire couldn't burn at night because the smoke would have given Jan away, it got almost cozy in the shed.

'I hope I'm doing the right thing,' said Steffens. 'I'm an old drunkard, 'Gina, but I like you. Just make sure you don't get caught.'

He was constantly drunk, sometimes a little more, sometimes a little less. It's possible he didn't even know what he was doing. And probably he did it as much for his son as for us. 'Children, children, so long as nothing happens to you,' he said, and left us pastry on the table in the shed.

I was with Jan almost every night. It was all so easy. Almost as though someone wanted to give us the present of those last few weeks.

Not even my mother could disturb us. She had moved in with my grandmother, in order to care for her. My grandmother who had never been sick! Now of all times she slipped on a potato peel in her own kitchen. The hospital had no empty beds. She had a cast put on and was brought home.

'You could come along to Granny's, Regine,' my mother suggested.

But I refused. 'Where would I study? In the living room, while the two of you talked about what you used to cook in peacetime?' I asked, and my mother agreed. She even thought it best for me to stay home and watch the apartment. My mother left. I stayed. When she returned four weeks later, they had already taken Jan and me away.

It had all been so easy. I waited until the air alert was over. Or until I thought there wouldn't be an alert. I went across the terrace and through the front garden, and, when the area seemed safe, I ran to the shed.

Jan waited. Jan opened the door. Jan closed it again.

'*Moje kochanie. Moje kochanie.*'

The oil lamp burned. The windows were draped. Our haven.

But I was always afraid.

'Would it be better for us to stop?' asked Jan. 'Not meet anymore? The war can't last much longer. If we can wait until then . . .'

'How much longer will the war last?'

'Three months. Four. At most six. Certainly no longer.'

'And if it does last longer?'

'It won't last longer.'

'Six months? I couldn't bear it.'

'And if I were a soldier?'

'I couldn't bear that, either.'

'One can bear so much, *kochanie*.'

'Could you bear it?'

He put his arms around me.

'Not today. Maybe tomorrow.'

'Yes,' I said. 'Tomorrow.'

We said it every night: Not today. Tomorrow.

Always tomorrow. Until there was no more tomorrow.

We lie in the shed and are afraid.

We listen.

What was that?

'Nothing, *moje kochanie*. It's only the wind.'
But one day it isn't the wind. It's footsteps. The
door opens. They come and take us away.
I hear them dragging Jan across the floor.
Where did they take him?
I open my eyes and am lying in the attic. The
bed, the chair, the window with the muslin cur-
tains, the whitewashed, cracked ceiling above me.
I'm so alone. I don't think I'll ever see him again.

I can't stand it. Always the same images. I don't
want to think anymore, to think about it from morning to night. I make up crossword puzzles, write
out French and English vocabulary, translate whole
pages, try to remember poems. I learned so many
poems by heart once. But I can barely get one of
them complete, a couple of lines are always missing.
Only two have come back to me whole.

The first was, of all things, the St. Nicholas poem
that I had had to recite year after year, even though
we had left the church:

> *I come from afar, from the forests so drear,*
> *I come to tell you all, Christmas is near.*
> *Everywhere, everywhere deep in the pines*
> *I saw golden lights that glimmer and shine.*
> *And there far above, from Heaven's bright shrine*
> *The Christ child peered forth at Christmas time . . .*

Not long ago, on Maurice's birthday, I recited it
with gusto over gooseberry wine. It was a great
success.

'Wonderful!' said Maurice. 'I have to take that back to France with me. Does your *Führer* know it? Perhaps he learned it as a child.'

The second poem I remember is by Rilke. In the months before Jan came, I had what Doris called a Rilke fetish. Rilke poems whatever I did, wherever I went. I only remember one, though:

A night in distant motion, for the train
of army baggage rolled past copse and lawn.
Yet he raised his eyes from the harpsichord's strain
and gazed at her while his fingers played on,

as though to catch an image mirrored there:
overflowing with the youth of his face
and knowing how sorrow would leave its trace,
more seductive and note by note more fair.

But all that suddenly faded away.
she stood as if drawn in the window bay
and stuggled to bring her heart to a lull.

His music stopped. A cool wind was playing.
And by the mirror, utterly changed, lay
the black shako with crossed bones and the skull.

Strange it should have been that particular poem. I must have liked it especially well.

I say it out loud to myself. They mean nothing to me – those higher beings with their harpsichord. What is a harpsichord, anyway? At the time, when I could still do it, I didn't even look it up in the dictionary. The pretty sound satisfied me. That perfectly rhymed farewell.

To a lull. And the skull.

I think of Jan and me. No freshness for us from copse or lawn. It was cold in the shed because we couldn't light the stove, and what we heard were footsteps creeping up through Steffens's garden. No, our farewell was not poetic. Blood ran from Jan's nose, and he moaned.

Chapter Fourteen

Mid-March. There's much more activity on the village street – equipment on its way to the fields for the spring planting. Fertilizing, harrowing, sowing – just like in the song we learned as children: 'In March-time the farmer his horsies teams . . .'

There are no more horsies at Henninghof, though, just a pair of ancient plow hacks. The good horses have long since been taken.

'And have probably long since dropped,' says Gertrud. 'Well, everything's going to hell, why not our horses.' She and Maurice get up at five in the morning and slave until it's dark. I'd like to help them, at least to work in the garden or the stable. I could put on a kerchief. There are evacuees and people who have been bombed out of their homes on almost every farm; probably no one would notice me.

But Gertrud doesn't want it.

'That's all we need,' she says. 'Now, right at the

end. You stay upstairs, Regine, and watch from inside. At least there's no shooting in your room.'

There was shooting out in the fields – strafers that suddenly appeared from beyond the forest. No one had expected that kind of attack, and suddenly there they were, firing machine guns at anything that moved. When they disappeared, old Wittkau lay dead beside his horse.

'Now we have the war in Gutwegen,' Gertrud said bitterly, when she and Maurice returned earlier than usual from the fields. 'And we're so out of the way here. Not even on a proper road.'

'Planes don't need a road,' said Maurice. 'And if Gutwegen suffers nothing worse than a couple of low-level attacks, you can consider yourselves lucky.'

Maurice, too, was pale and upset. He yelled at the dog when it sprang up to greet him, and hardly ate any supper, although Gertrud said over and over: 'Come on, eat. You can starve in peacetime if you want.'

Peacetime. What a phrase. Is there such a thing as peace?

The Russians have reached Stettin, the Americans have captured Cologne. Appeals come over Radio London every evening to the German people, urging them to surrender without a struggle.

'Don't resist. Put out white flags! The war is over. Avoid unnecessary bloodshed.'

But the German radio still sends out rallying cries.

No mention of the refugees, the bombed-out sur-
vivors, the collapse on all fronts. Talk only of a
heroic battle to the last cartridge. And, of course, of
the miracle weapons that will shortly be ready.

'*We will reconquer every meter of our blood-soaked
homeland . . .*'

Last night we heard it again. Hans Fritzsche and
his drivel.

'I'll wring that one's neck,' said Gertrud and
turned off the radio. 'Can anyone really still believe
that?'

I think about my mother. Surely she, too, was
sitting by the radio.

I visited her in October, when she was caring for
my grandmother. We had a conversation – our last.

'Mama,' I said to her then, 'You finally have to
realize that . . .'

But she plugged her ears.

'If that's true,' she said. 'If we've been so wrong
. . . No, it's not true. We can't be that wrong. How
could we go on living?'

My grandmother's apartment lies in the northern
part of the city. 'The workers' quarter,' my mother
calls it, although she and my father grew up there.

My grandmother was lying on the sofa when I
arrived. Her face looked even thinner and more
severe against the red velvet.

'The longer you're in bed, the sicker you get,' she

said. 'It starts with your leg, it stops with your heart. Maybe it's better this way. Who knows what lies ahead of us.'

'Do be quiet,' my mother said, depressed.

'Why, what's wrong?' I asked.

My mother pulled a sheet of paper out of her apron pocket, unfolded it and passed it to me.

NAZI PIGS, it said. In big, red letters.

A gallows had been drawn underneath, with a stick man dangling from it.

'Now they're coming back out of their holes, those Reds,' said my mother. 'They've knuckled under until now. They used to be happy if Papa would put in a good word for them.'

'They were plain jealous of you,' said my grandmother. 'A good thing Father hasn't lived to see this.'

My mother stared at the sheet of paper.

'It was probably that Schneider,' she said. 'She wouldn't forget.'

'Forget what?' I asked.

'That they picked her husband up in thirty-three.'

Mrs. Schneider lived a couple of houses farther down. Her two daughters were about my age.

'But why?' I asked. 'Why did they pick him up?'

'Because he was a Communist,' said my mother.

'Did he come back?' I asked.

My mother shrugged her shoulders.

'He died in prison,' said my grandmother. 'He had lung trouble anyway.'

'Don't stare at me like that,' said my mother. 'I can't do anything about it. Do you think I didn't pity him? And his wife . . . I went to school with her.'

She put away the note.

'It was his own fault. He was an enemy of the state. And we had to rebuild Germany.'

'We!' I said. 'Listen to that. We! It makes me sick!'

My grandmother sat up.

'Don't be fresh with your mother.'

'Rebuild! We! And if we lose the war and others want to rebuild Germany and if they come and pick you up because to them you're an enemy of the state, then *that's* a crime, right?'

My mother didn't answer. And then I began to tell her what I'd heard on Radio London. How things really stood with the war. What exactly had happened in the occupied lands. About the concentration camps . . .

'You're listening to enemy broadcasts!' she said. 'I leave you by yourself, and you listen to enemy broadcasts. Anyway, how do you know . . . I forbid it.'

I told her she couldn't stop me anymore.

'But they're lying!' she cried. 'They're *lying*!'

'And the others claim we're being lied to here. Who's telling the truth?'

'The *Führer* wouldn't do a thing like that,' she said.

'And where have all the Jews in Germany gone?' I asked. 'Even I know how many we had in Steinbergen. Dobrin. And Kulp. And Dänemark. And Löwenthal. Lena Kulp and Sally Löwenthal were in my class. Where are they all?'

She put her hands to her ears.

'It's not true!'

'Yes, it is!' I screamed. 'The whole world knows it. And you cover your ears!'

'The Jews ruined Germany,' she said.

I started crying.

'Mama,' I said. 'You aren't really like that . . .'

We were both crying, and she said. 'If it's true . . . if we've been so wrong . . . then how can we go on? It just can't be true.'

That's how I saw my mother the last time: she sat at the table and covered her ears.

'And at the same time, she's really a very nice lady,' Gertrud said. 'I'm sure she wouldn't hurt a fly.'

'No, not my mother. On the contrary. Whenever someone needed help among our neighbors, she was always there. And if a Jewish child had crossed her path . . .'

'She probably would have given him something to eat.' Gertrud nodded. 'Sure, that's how good people are. But talking like a fool is just as bad, unfortunately. Couldn't she just *think* once in a while?'

'Not everyone is as sharp as you, *chérie*,' said Maurice. 'It's a very complicated thing. We'll be thinking about this for a long time to come.'

'We?' Gertrud looked at him. 'I keep hearing we. Not you, certainly. You're a Frenchman.'

'All of us,' said Maurice.

Yesterday, in the middle of the day, there was another aerial attack on Steinbergen. They hit St. Peter's School. It stands in the quarter where my grandmother lives, right near her.

Has anything happened to my grandmother?

The idea that I may never see her again hardly bothers me. I never liked her much anyway. I was only attached to my grandfather, my grandfather with his workshop that smelled of wood, my grandfather who told me stories. Made-up stories mostly about Hansi Longears, a big white rabbit. My grandfather was crazy about rabbits. Out back in the courtyard stood the cages, screened wooden crates full of gray rabbits. Only Hansi Longears, the hero of our stories, was white.

My grandfather has been dead a long time.

'A good thing Father didn't live to see this,' my grandmother would say when she was angry about something. And she was angry constantly.

I see her before me, my grandmother with her navy-blue coat and navy-blue hat over her bun. Before she got married she was a servant for an associate regional court judge: 'Very distinguished people. And his missus always had a hat and veil and a navy-blue coat . . .'

That's why my grandmother wears navy-blue coats. One for Sundays, one for everyday. She airs and brushes it every time before she puts it back in the wardrobe. My grandmother is withered and strict and so frugal that she even hoards her salt.

'She had to be,' said my mother. 'Pappy could only work a few hours at a time because of his rheumatism. And during the bad days they had us on their necks as well, and everything still had to be orderly.'

Orderly. The word cropped up in every other sentence with my grandmother.

Look orderly.

An orderly apartment.

An orderly person.

During the lean years she leased a garden outside the city. We had to work there every day, even I, so that it would 'look orderly' and 'produce properly.' We had to pull up weeds, collect stones, pick berries, pull out onions. . . . The garden was much too big, but we lived off it. When my grandfather died in 1935 and my grandmother started having heart trouble, my parents were supposed to take it over.

That was one of the few occasions on which my mother rebelled against her.

'Never!' she cried. 'No more garden,' at which

point my grandmother no doubt responded with her favorite saying: Pride goeth before a fall.

She repeated it countless times after the war began. And surely after my arrest.

She may even have been right. If we had kept the garden, I wouldn't have gone to Steffens, I wouldn't have met Jan, I wouldn't be sitting here in the attic, my mother wouldn't have to think me dead.

Who could have betrayed us? Not Steffens. Steffens was arrested the same night. That only leaves Feldmann, really.

I never said a word about Jan and me, not to anyone, not even to Doris. Though I would have liked to so much when the days between the nights seemed endless and I could hardly bear the fear and the happiness and the doubt.

Those short nights. What did I know about Jan anyway? I knew his voice, his face, his body. I fantasized a complete Jan for myself. But was it the real one?

The Jan I know is affectionate and soft-hearted. He doesn't hate. He doesn't want revenge. He never says: 'The Germans killed my father.' He says: 'It was a couple of murderers. And when this war is over, we'll have to start all over again. Anyone who doesn't want this to happen again. You'll have to help, too.'

'But how?' I ask.

'Talk to people. Explain to them what we know.'

'When I think of my mother . . .' I say. 'Would she understand it?'

'You have to explain it to her properly, then she'll understand. You and I have seen something; we have to pass it on to others, so that they can see it, too. That must become our path. Every person has to lay a path.'

We talk about so many things every night. But do you get to know a person that way?

We talked about that, too.

'What will you do after the war, Jan? Will you go away?'

'I have to go home. Home to Cracow.'

'And what about me?'

'I don't know, *moje kochanie*. I'd like to take you along. But I don't know if I can. There will be a lot of hatred after the war.'

'What should we do?'

'Not forget anything, Regina.'

'I won't, Jan. Will you forget me?'

'I don't want to. But time does funny things.'

'Why do you say that?'

'Because I don't want to make a promise I may not be able to keep. We only see each other at night . . .'

I get up. I want to leave, but he holds me fast.

'If we are the way we are now, we won't forget anything. Then you'll come to me, or I to you, and we'll live.'

116

'But aren't we living now, Jan?'

'Yes, we're living. But only halfway. The night isn't life. Life is working and eating together and having friends and going swimming and to the movies and being sick and fighting and making up. I'd like to live with you.'

'And I with you, Jan.'

But there's only enough time for us to love each other. Jan is right, it isn't enough. And yet so much that I wait all day for evening to come. When I'm with him everything is all right.

'Lay a path,' Jan said.

Maurice likes that.

'I'll remember that,' he says. 'Lay a path. Later, when I'm a teacher again in France, I'm going to think about that. And that, too, will be your Jan's path.'

'And I'll be nothing again,' says Gertrud. 'I'll lay a path in the field. For beans.'

Maurice shakes his head.

'You yourself are a path, *chérie*,' he says, and Gertrud goes red.

And I? What path will I lay when I get out of here?

'You've learned so much,' says Maurice. 'Something will occur to you.'

I don't know anymore if chemistry is the right thing for me.

I want to work with people. To learn something about people, to do something with people.

'Formulae and vocabularies are not that important. Why people are the way they are, that's what you have to know.'

Jan had said that, too. He made me think of so many new things, brought so many new ideas to light. But the time was always too short.

Yes, I would have liked to talk to Doris about Jan. I needed it. To sit opposite her in her room after school, to say it out loud, to hear my voice and how it sounds his name: His name is Jan. We meet almost every night.

I started to tell her a couple of times.

'You know, Doris, I . . .'

But I never got any further. I wasn't sure what she really thought, not then, not now.

And then there was her father's fiftieth birthday.

'You're invited,' she said. 'As Wolf's dinner partner.'

Wolf, her cousin – I knew him from when he was a boy and spent the holidays with the Weisskopfs. When he looked at you, he raised his eyebrows almost to the roots of his hair. Now he was a lieutenant, an antitank gunner, badly wounded. I couldn't decline. But I would rather have gone to Jan.

'Put on your white dress,' said Doris. 'It will be a real party.'

From the beginning I had the feeling I didn't belong at that party. The gentlemen mostly in uniform, the ladies in long dresses, candlelight (where did they get all the candles?), two girls in white aprons serving drinks on silver trays.

Mrs. Weisskopf welcomes me at the door. I know her well; I've even watched her cook. Tonight, in her black velvet dress, she is ceremonious and distant in a pompous way.

'I'd like to present Doris's friend Regine,' she says to the room at large. 'As reinforcements for the younger generation. Regine, this is General Hoffmann.'

She moves with me from one guest to another – uniforms, medals, evening gowns.

Even Dr. Weisskopf is wearing a uniform and a decoration. My father is just a private. My friend a Polish slave worker. How does one talk to a general?

Wolf, the lieutenant, clicks his heels: 'If I may be allowed to remind the General, sir . . .'

It's like a movie. I think of Jochen Creutzer, of the farmer's wife, of Walter Henning. How many millions have already died in this war? I think of Jan and myself and would like to leave.

'Well, our 'Gina,' says Wolf. 'So grown up!'

'If I may be permitted to remind the Lieutenant, sir, that I'm not ten anymore,' I say.

He raises his eyebrows as high as he used to, looks at me, and laughs. Over dinner he tells me he's been in the hospital for seven months with a lung wound and all sorts of other complications.

'I had begun to hope the war was over for me,' he says. 'And now I have to go back after all.'

'Perhaps the General, sir, will put in a good word

for you,' I murmur, and he laughs again and says: 'You really have grown up.'

We sit at the lavish table and eat. There's soup, fish, chicken fricassee – all the things I know now only from Mother's cookbook. The presumption with which they are passed around, served, and eaten, makes me more and more mulish. I'm hungry, but I hardly eat anything. I'd like to be with Jan. These people around the table are his enemies. *My* enemies. I don't want to eat with them.

And then I hear the lady across from me say: 'Those faces. Simply animal.'

She is talking about the Russian POWs. I saw them, a gray mass, probably on the march to another camp, ragged and gaunt.

It was noon when I met them, not far from the factory on the outskirts of the city. And I saw a woman run after them and give the last one a chunk of bread. A dried-up woman, like my grandmother. She surely knew how dangerous it was to do what she was doing.

And this female at the table says: 'Simply animal.'

I can't stand it anymore.

'They're not animals,' I say. 'They're people just like us.'

It's the same as it was with the school essay. I have to get it out.

Wolf grasps my arm as though to pull me back,

then lets me go. It grows still. I see faces, hands with forks in the air, no movement, like in Sleeping Beauty after she pricks herself on the spindle. And finally the voice of Dr. Weisskopf: 'Regine, I must ask you not to mention the Russians and us in the same breath in my house.'

Voices rise again, forks dig into the chicken fricassee, wine is poured.

I want to get up, but Wolf holds me fast.

'Don't do it,' he says softly.

After the meal I go out into the vestibule. Mrs. Weisskopf follows me.

'Did that have to happen, Regine?' she asks angrily. 'At your age you ought to know what can and cannot be said.'

I don't answer.

'I guess you've gone crazy,' says Doris. 'How else could my father react? With all these people here? You never know . . .'

'Shut your mouth,' her mother threatens her, and I wait until they leave me alone, then put on my coat and go.

With all these people here . . .

What did Doris mean by that? Doesn't her father trust his guests? Which side is he on? Should one fear him?

Or is he himself afraid?

Doris, her father, her mother – could you trust them? I was happy Doris knew nothing about Jan and me.

121

'Some people will talk their heads into a noose,' Steffens scolded when he heard the story. 'There are informers hanging around everywhere. It only takes one to prick up his ears and think: That little one there, we ought to watch her more closely – and then he's off to Feldmann and asks this and that and hears that you like to go for walks in the evening . . .'

'Feldmann has never seen me yet,' I said. 'I've been careful.'

But it was true: Informers lurked everywhere. In Steinbergen a woman who owned a dairy store had just been arrested. One morning when her shop was full of people, she had received the news of her son's death. With the letter in her hand she burst into the shop: 'He's dead!' she screamed. 'He's dead. This damned war. Damn Hitler! He killed him!'

A couple of women hurried her out of the shop and closed the door behind her. You could still hear her screaming. That afternoon she was picked up. Taken away.

Miss Rosius is gone, too.

After Doris and I visited her, she no longer said 'Be seated,' but '*Heil* Hitler' instead, though never very clearly. It sounded like 'Heiler' or 'Hiller' – which was pretty standard. Most people drew the syllables together, that happens when you use a word frequently. But Ilse Mattfeld said:

'She doesn't want to. You can tell.'

'I think you're mad at her because you got a five,' said Doris, and Ilse Mattfeld returned:

'Funny how you always defend her.'

Then Doris kept quiet.

Another biology class. Ethnology again.

'It has in no way been scientifically proven that the Nordic race has special advantages,' Miss Rosius says. 'There are numerous important people with distinctly Oriental characteristics.'

The next day, she didn't come to school.

Two Gestapo agents appeared instead, set themselves up in the headmaster's office, and called us in one after another for questioning.

'I don't know a thing,' Doris said to me before she went in. 'I was thinking of my dead boyfriend.'

I came after her.

The two Gestapo men looked at me with a fatherly air. They were older men. One was thin and sick-looking, the other had a paunch and a round, good-natured face. He could have been a baker.

'You are Regine Martens?' he asked, and smiled kindly. 'Your father is a comrade in the party?'

'Yes,' I said. 'Has been since 1930.'

'We know that,' he said. 'And so you can also tell us, I'm sure, what Assistant Schoolmistress Rosius said about the Nordic race in the last biology class.'

I shook my head. No, I couldn't do that. I had been learning French vocabulary. I only knew what the others had told me later.

'That's too bad,' said the fat one. 'Your friend

Doris Weisskopf wasn't listening, either. What is your grade in biology, incidentally?'

'A two,' I said. My palms were damp, as they always are when I'm scared. There were big wet patches on my blouse under my arms. The fat one noted them with interest.

'A two?' said the thin one. 'Even though you don't pay attention?'

'Usually I do,' I said. 'But that day I didn't know my vocabulary because I had hospital duty the afternoon before.'

'I see,' he said. 'Hospital duty? Did Assistant Schoolmistress Rosius give the Hitler salute?'

I said 'yes' and was allowed to go.

'They were satisfied with that?' Maurice was amazed. 'Really nice people, the Gestapo,' Gertrud offered.

'What do you mean?' I said. 'Isn't it believable that you might learn vocabulary during biology class once in a while? And they must have had enough other statements. Rosius never came back anyway.'

'She was as cracked as you and your essay,' said Gertrud. 'And your "Russians are people, too." Now she's probably tearing her hair. If she still can.'

At school, we were told she'd been transferred for disciplinary reasons. I had a chemistry book she'd loaned me, and asked Dr. Mühlhoff for her new address.

'I don't have it,' he said.

'Can I get the address from the headmaster's office?' I asked.

'If I were you I'd forget it.'

Steffens was right. There were informers everywhere. You only had to move over to the other side to discover it.

Was I too careless?

I sit in the attic and feel that fear again. It gets worse and worse, like a tumor growing inside me.

In the cellar they had spoken of a farmer's daughter from Rodingen who was caught with a Pole.

'They cut off her hair,' said Mrs. Lieberecht, whose sister lives in Rodingen. 'Off with her hair and into the stocks with her for a whole day. And then the Gestapo took her away.'

Silence. And in the silence Feldmann's voice: 'They ought to hang whores like that. No shilly-shallying. Hang them right off.'

That night I hardly dared go out. Shortly before half past eleven there was an air alert. At quarter to twelve came the all clear. I waited more than an hour, until there wasn't a sound to be heard in the house. Only then did I slip into the street. I looked around after every step. No, nothing. No shadow, no sound. When I finally reached Jan's, I was shaking.

'It's cold out,' I said.

'You mustn't come anymore,' said Jan. 'You won't hold up. And you're not sleeping enough.'

'I sleep in the afternoons,' I said.

He put me on the sofa, covered me, sat by me. I feel his fingers on my face, they run over my forehead, my nose, my chin, my throat. The lamp flickers. His eyes are so clear. I see only his eyes.

'We should stop while it's good, *moje kochanie*,' he whispers.

'A sensible boy, your Jan,' says Gertrud. 'You should have listened to him.'

But I don't think he really wanted it. We said goodbye on that evening. We called it a goodbye. But everything Jan did meant simply: Come again.

'Yes, yes, *ma petite*,' said Maurice. 'A mouth can talk and talk.'

Maurice is worried. A couple of his friends who work on neighboring farms want to escape to the English, who are already in Osnabrück.

'They're crazy,' says Maurice. 'Now of all times, right at the end! If they get caught, they'll be hanged, and we others will suffer for it. Why run to the English? They're coming to us of their own accord.'

From the west the Americans and the English, from the east the Russians. Everything is collapsing. Gertrud says Steinbergen is overflowing with refu- gees. They sleep in schools, dance halls, movie houses. Endless columns block the highways, farm- ers who have left their villages and farms to the east with no more than what will fit in their horse carts.

They flee from the approaching front, from the Russians. Terrible things are being reported, everyone speaks of looting, rape, executions.

'Now they're getting upset,' says Maurice.

'But what happened in Russia?'

'No one is running away from the Americans,' says Gertrud, and Maurice looks at her and shakes his head and argues that you can't really compare the two.

'The Russians, they had the war in their homeland. And what a war! The German offensive, the occupation, then the retreat. Now as they march into Germany they see burned villages and hear about everything that has happened. If I were a Russian, who knows what I'd do.'

He falls silent, stirs his peppermint tea.

'Hate only produces hatred. This war is far from over. It will go on, even when there's no more shooting. You'll remember my words.'

The farmers in Gutwegen fear not only the Russians, but the refugees as well.

'When they get to a village, they act as though everything belonged to them' – or so you hear, and Maurice shakes his head and says: 'Everyone gets to eat, but now the other guy's supposed to pay.'

But the columns pass Gutwegen by. We lie too far out of the way. The road that turns off the highway and leads through woods and fields isn't even tarred.

'Oh God, oh God,' Gertrud moans. 'Will we have to leave, too?'

'Where would you like to go?' asks Maurice. 'Stay where you are and wait it out.'

'And what will the Russians do to us?'

'Have you done anything to them?' asks Maurice.

'As though that's what matters, when the world's upside down,' says Gertrud. Maurice runs his fingers through her hair, which has already begun to bleach out.

'Besides, I'm still here. I'll take care of you.'

Gertrud angrily pushes away his hand.

'You can kiss them on the nose,' she says. 'Maybe they'll like that.'

Chapter Fifteen

UPSTAIRS in the attic. I stand at the open window and see nothing. A night in black cotton. Silence and darkness, only the animals stir occasionally. The noise seems odd, as though it didn't belong.

The farmer's wife is dead.

Yesterday morning she was still alive. Now she lies on her bed in the black dress with a black kerchief, her hands folded over the Bible. She looks, as always, serious and withdrawn. Her face had long seemed made of stone.

In the morning she came to see me once more. Gertrud and Maurice were turning the soil in the garden when I heard her footsteps on the stairs. She sat down, was silent, said finally: 'Today we'll have milk soup with dumplings and boiled potatoes with sauce for lunch,' was quiet again, and then asked her question.

I gave my answer, and she said: 'And not one of them in the cemetery here. Four sons and not a single grave.'

I said that, at the end of the previous war, the dead had been brought home, but she didn't answer. She sat a while longer, then stood up and left.

Later, Gertrud brought me the milk soup and boiled potatoes. 'There's been another raid on Steinbergen,' she said. 'This time the train station got it. And they say the sugar factory took a hit as well.'

'And the cannery?' I asked.

'Teltow didn't hear anything about that,' she said. 'I'll ride in tomorrow and check.' She went to the door. 'Anyway, I have to see if I can't come up with some drops for Mother's heart condition.'

At that moment, we heard the sound of a motor.

'I think there's a car coming,' said Gertrud.

We stood behind the curtains and watched a military vehicle drive into the village. It was an open jeep carrying four soldiers.

'What do they want?' Gertrud whispered. Her fingers dug into my arm. 'You've got to hide. Run to the loft.'

I went completely empty with fear. I couldn't move. I stood behind the curtain and stared out. This was what I had feared, in the mornings on waking, in the evenings before going to sleep, and every minute in between. That someone would see and betray me, that they would come to get me. Like the first time.

The jeep stopped. Not in front of our house, but farther down by the Kruses'. The soldiers jumped out. Two ran into Krusehof, two remained at the gate, guns ready in their hands. Gertrud let go of my arm.

'They aren't coming here,' she whispered.

'They still may,' I whispered back.

I wanted to do what Gertrud had said, run to the loft and crawl into the hiding place Maurice had set up right at the beginning. But I couldn't move my legs, as though there were no connection between them and my head.

'Here they are again,' Gertrud whispered.

I saw the uniforms at the farm door and thought: Now they'll come and get me.

Then I heard the screams. A woman's voice.

'Fritz! Fritz! Fritz!' she screamed, and I saw the young man who was walking between the two soldiers. They held him fast, he had lowered his head, and the screaming woman was Mrs. Kruse. She ran after them.

'Fritz!' she screamed. On and on just 'Fritz!'

'Oh God,' whispered Gertrud. 'It's Fritz Kruse!'

The soldiers shoved him into the jeep.

Mrs. Kruse rushed after him, screaming, clinging to him. He raised his head and said something, and the others tore her away from him and shoved her aside. I saw her stumble, heard the sound of the engine, saw the jeep pull away, heard Mrs. Kruse scream again. Someone came, picked her up, took her into the house. No more screams, just the motor. It grew fainter, faded away in the distance.

'They're gone,' said Gertrud and let herself fall on the chair. 'Fritz Kruse . . .'

She closed her eyes and pounded a fist against her forehead.

'How dumb can you get. Hides at home, of all places. Where they'll look for him first off. And old Mrs. Dagelmann right next door.'

'What will they do to him?' I asked, and thought of Jan, whom they had also picked up, Jan and me, each in a separate car.

The black car in which Jan disappeared . . .

'A deserter,' said Gertrud. 'What do they do to a deserter? Oh God, and the war is almost over.'

The farmer's wife read from the Bible again that evening. Later, I saw it was Psalm 13.

' "How long must I bear pain in my soul, and have sorrow in my heart all the day?" ' she read, and we sat around the table and were still. Her eyes were puffy. She ran her finger beneath the lines, faltering and uncertain, as though she found it difficult to decipher the words.

She had cried a long time that afternoon.

'For the first time,' said Gertrud. 'With our boys she didn't get a single tear out. And suddenly it starts with Fritz Kruse. Mind you, she couldn't stand him, he was such a brat. Well, now she's mourned them all together. It's good it's out.'

'"How long shall my enemy be exalted over me? Consider and answer me, O Lord my God,"' the farmer's wife read, and I thought of the many people who, like her, were praying for help at that moment – perhaps Fritz Kruse as well, perhaps even Jan. And I thought about what I would be doing now if they had picked me up instead of Fritz Kruse, and what it was like when I prayed for help in prison. And I thought that I wouldn't be able to stand it much longer; day after day and every day they say the war is coming to an end, but it goes on and on with me here at Henninghof until they come again and get me.

It will never end, I thought, never, never. The words pounded in my head like a hammer, and over it all the voice of the farmer's wife: '"Lighten my eyes, lest I sleep the sleep of death; lest my enemy say, 'I have prevailed over him . . .'"'

I began to cry.

'It will never end,' I sobbed. 'It will never end. It will never end.'

'Come,' said Gertrud. 'Drink something.'

She poured me a cup of peppermint tea. I took the cup and drank.

The farmer's wife was mute. She sat there, the Bible open in her hands, looking at the photographs on the wall.

Then she laid the Bible on the table and stood up heavily.

133

'At least we've always had enough to eat,' she said, in a voice that sounded very odd and metallic. She took a few steps toward the door, heaved a gurgling sigh, and collapsed.

Maurice rushed to catch her, but she already lay on the ground.

'Mother!' Gertrud screamed.

Maurice knelt by the farmer's wife. He put his ear to her chest, raised her hand, let it fall, and with a gentle motion ran his hand over her eyes.

Gertrud was still sitting in her place. Maurice stood up and put his arms around her.

'It was a good death, *chérie*,' he said.

Gertrud looked at him blankly.

'A good death,' Maurice repeated softly.

'Oh?' said Gertrud.

She freed herself from Maurice, went over to her mother, stood by her for a while, then turned to Maurice and said: 'A good life wouldn't have been a bad thing, either.'

Later, we carried the farmer's wife to her bed. I fetched the Bible in order to lay it on her chest. I noticed then that she had been reading the thirteenth psalm.

That night we stayed with her to keep the vigil.

Gertrud had moved the chairs up to the bed. She sat at the head, then came Maurice, then me. A candle burned on the night table.

'We've got five,' said Gertrud. 'Maybe they'll last till tomorrow morning.'

I had never been in that room before. The farmer's wife had always made her own bed. It was a low room, whitewashed and with two small windows. There were the marriage beds, a wardrobe, a bureau, a chest, and it took some time before I could inhale the odor without distaste – such a heavy, sharp smell of old wood, sweaty clothes, urine. The house had been standing nearly two hundred years. I thought of the people who had lain in the beds, of the many children who had been born, of the many who had died. Perhaps every one of them had left a bit of his odor behind.

We sat by her bed in silence. I looked into the still, stony face and realized for the first time what it means to be dead, not to be alive anymore. I thought of the lock of hair in the wedding picture, and of how young the farmer's wife had been, of how she had laughed, and of the many years between then and now. I thought of the time she had put behind her and of the time that lay ahead for me. My years. My time. The farmer's wife was dead, but I was young, I was alive, and I would have liked to jump up and run, anywhere, just to feel it – living.

'When will the war be over?' I said into the stillness, and Gertrud started crying, loudly and without restraint, like a small child.

Maurice didn't try to comfort her. He let her cry, and after a while she stopped.

135

The second candle burned down. I got tired, slept, woke up again. Every quarter-hour we heard the chime of the wall clock in the parlor. Eleven, twelve, one.

'Another five hours,' said Gertrud. 'At six I'll fetch the neighbors.'

She went into the kitchen and returned with a tray. She had brewed coffee and made sandwiches. We ate and drank.

'At least we've always had enough to eat,' said Maurice. 'Those were her last words.'

He went to the head of the bed and looked down at the face of the farmer's wife. 'When I came here,' he said, 'I was crazy with hatred. My country had been overrun by the Germans, my brother killed, I had to leave, leave my wife, my son, my work. I couldn't think, couldn't feel anything, only anger and hatred. And then she stood before me and looked at me and said: "What's your name? Moritz?" and showed me my room and made my bed. Made it – didn't just throw the sheets on the mattress. She gave me a place at the table and put the same thing on my plate as the others. She took me in and I belonged. And one day my hatred was gone. I didn't hate the Germans anymore. Only those who were really responsible for this war, but not *all* Germans, not anymore.'

Almost the same words as Jan's. A Pole, a Frenchman, the same words.

'She was a good mother, *chérie*,' said Maurice.

'She was a human being. And she made me a human being again.' He turned to me. 'How did your Jan put it? Lay a path? That's what she did. She laid a path.'

'Only it didn't do her any good,' said Gertrud.

'Maybe it did.' Maurice sat down again. 'What do we know?'

Time passed. Gertrud lit another candle. When the clock struck three, she said: 'Go to bed. I want to be alone with her.'

Chapter Sixteen

But I can't sleep. I stand at the window and let the night air in, as I do sometimes when it's this dark. March air. It smells of earth and damp meadows. I came in the fall, I'll go in the spring.

The farmer's wife is dead.

'She made me a human being again,' Maurice had said.

And I? What kind of human being have I become in the past six months? What will I be like when I come home again? When I see them again, Feldmann, the Hagemanns, the Frankes, the Lieberechts, Mrs. Bühler? One of them betrayed us, one of them is guilty. And the others stood by as they took us away. Stood by and approved it. The moon shone, I could see their faces. 'Pole's slut,' one of them yelled.

That horrible night.

I never believed they would come. I had feared

it, but never believed it. The way I can't imagine
growing old. Old like the farmer's wife. And dying.
Although I know everyone grows old and dies.

The twenty-fifth of October. A fall day, damp and
cloudy.

Horse carts full of sugar beets drove through the
streets to the Steinbergen sugar factory. Syrup was
being cooked at the cannery. A sweet, rotten odor
hung over the city.

I hadn't been with Jan in two nights. We wanted
to stop seeing each other. But we had said that
before and not kept to it. I tried to study physics in
the afternoon. But I couldn't do it – I thought of
Jan, of the coming cold that would make staying in
the shed much longer impossible. Winter was coming. It was getting cold. He would move in with
Steffens, into the room by the horse stall where, in
any case, he lived officially.

'The boy is freezing here,' said Steffens. 'He's
already coughing like the devil. You can still visit
us, 'Gina. And in the spring the whole nightmare
will be over, so then you'll finally be able to go
dancing together.'

Dancing. I would have liked so much to dance
with Jan. At least once. In my white dress with the
blue trim . . .

I knew in the afternoon I wanted to be with him
that night. I didn't wait to see if there would be an

alert. Soon after it got dark, I slipped out of the house.

The shed was locked. I knocked, short-long-long-short. That was our signal.

Jan opened the door. I saw he had been sleeping. He didn't look well and he coughed.

'Why have you come, Regina?' he asked. 'We had agreed not to anymore.'

There were beads of sweat on his forehead.

'Are you sick, Jan?' I asked.

'Go away,' he said. 'Please.'

I didn't answer. We stood facing each other. He hadn't kissed me yet. Now he reached out and pulled me to him.

'A Pole I know,' he said, 'one from the railway workshop – they hanged him yesterday. He had a German girlfriend, a married woman. I don't know what they did with the woman. But they hanged him from a tree in the courtyard.'

He let his head fall on my shoulder.

'He stood on the bed of a truck, and then they drove the truck out from under him. All the Poles who work in the shop had to watch. He had a sign around his neck: I have defiled Germany's honor.'

Jan spoke low and hastily. Every time he took a breath, he coughed.

'I'm afraid,' he said. 'I thought I could take it. But I can't. I don't want to die. The war will be over soon; then we can be together without danger.'

He kissed me. 'I know it's my fault. I started it. I should have left you in peace.'

'No,' I said. 'I started it just as much. I came back that time of my own free will. I didn't want it any other way.'

'It was good, *moje kochanie*,' he said. 'In spite of everything. Others maybe, they only play. Not us. We took a risk.'

He kissed me again, and I started to leave. But it was too late.

Jan raised his head. 'Someone's here,' he whispered.

I hadn't heard a thing. I only knew it when they broke in the door. Four men. Not policemen. Men in civilian clothes. Four dark figures. Four dark coats. Four dark hats. Pale circles under the hats.

Two of them grabbed me, held me fast.

'So, you pig,' said one of them. 'Does a Polack do it better than a German soldier?'

Then I heard a cry. It was Jan. The other two were slugging him. He fell to the ground, and they started to kick him. Blood ran from his nose.

'Lay off,' said one of the ones holding me. 'Otherwise he won't get anything out of swinging.'

Then they shoved me out of the shed, through the garden to the street. I heard Jan's footsteps dragging behind me. He moaned once.

Two black cars in front of the garden gate. Next to them, the people from our building. Maybe the Gestapo rang at our apartment first, pounded on the door, rounded up the tenants. Maybe they needed an audience. I don't know. But they were there. 'Pole's slut!' one of them yelled.

141

It had been very still. No one had spoken. And then those words.

The Gestapo agents shoved me forward.

'Is this Martens?' asked one.

'Yes,' said Feldmann. He stood with his wife in the first row, next to Lisabeth Hagemann.

'What shall we do with her?' asked the Gestapo agent.

No one answered.

'Then let's start with this,' he said.

He grabbed my hair, pulled it. I cried out, it hurt so much. Then I saw the scissors. 'No!' I wanted to scream. But the scream got stuck. And when it finally came out, the man held my braid in his hand. 'Who wants it?' he asked, and threw it at the people's feet. Then he cut the rest of my hair off, right along my scalp.

'That's what a Pole's slut looks like,' he said. 'Now let's go. Off with you.'

They dragged me into the car. The other car had already gone. With Jan. I hadn't noticed them taking Jan away.

The ride through the city – I recall none of it. My memory only begins at the point where the car stopped.

'Get out,' said the Gestapo agent.

We stood in front of the prison near the cathedral. The big red building with the wall and all the windows. I had walked by it so often. Others had been kept there, lawbreakers, criminal types, social parasites.

Now I was one of them.

'We'll come for you tomorrow,' the Gestapo agents said before they left.

The uniformed guard who took me to my cell was old and white-haired. Even his eyebrows were white.

He opened the cell door. I saw the plank bed, the barred window, the bucket in the corner . . .

'Well, go in,' said the guard.

I heard how weary his voice sounded. I heard everything, saw everything, observed everything much more clearly than usual.

'Lie down,' said the guard. 'Perhaps you'll sleep.'

He had dark eyes under his white eyebrows, almost black.

'How old are you?' he asked.

'Seventeen,' I said.

He shook his head and sighed.

'Did this have to happen?' he asked.

I was silent.

He sighed again.

'What should I do?' I asked.

'Pray,' he said.

'And did you pray?' asked Gertrud, when I spoke of that night.

'One doesn't ask that.' Maurice wanted to set her straight, and Gertrud got irritated.

'One doesn't ask, one doesn't ask. Are we such

refined people we can't ask that? It happens to be important. Because if she did in fact pray, she got results. I never did. So, did you pray?' I nodded my head.

'Maybe you were lucky,' said Gertrud. 'And I wasn't. I prayed so much! First, that nothing would happen to my brothers. Then, that three would come back, or two. And at the end, that they would only blow off one of Walter's legs, or an arm. All for nothing.'

She looked defiantly at me and Maurice.

'It's obvious, anyway, it can't work. After all, I'm not the only one who's had the idea. Every mother and sister and girlfriend prays for her boy, all at the same time. And the grenades have to explode somewhere; they don't just vanish into thin air. So who should they get? And who not? If you ask me – I wouldn't want to be the heavenly Father. I . . .'

'Don't say that, *chérie*,' Maurice broke in.

'It's true, isn't it?' Gertrud asked.

I had never seen her so angry. Her face was burning like it did during the rye harvest in August.

'No, it isn't true,' said Maurice.

'Why not?' asked Gertrud.

'Because you want to lay down the rules,' said Maurice. 'You demand something and get mad when you don't receive it. Instead of saying: "Do what is right."'

'Ah!' said Gertrud. She stuck her head forward and gazed at Maurice in confusion. 'Then it must be right for all our boys to be dead?'

Maurice put his arm around her. I turned my head away, it looked so loving.

'*Chérie*,' he said. 'It's terrible for you. But for your brothers – what it is for them – can you say?'

Gertrud's face still bore the same expression.

'Maurice,' she said. 'You sure are devout!'

He smiled.

'Perhaps. After all, your mother reads us psalms every night.'

It is beginning to grow light in the attic. I close the window and lie down on the bed. But I can't sleep. I think about the night they picked me up. I close my eyes and am lying once again on the plank bed. I breathe the stench coming from the corner with the cell w.c., feel the scratchy blanket and the moonlight on my eyelids.

'Pray,' the guard had said.

Yes, I prayed that night. Not right away. I wasn't used to it. When I was small, my mother had taught me how. 'Dearest God, make me good, I long for heaven as good girls should.' Or: 'I am little, my heart is clear, no one shall live there but Jesus dear.' Every night before I went to sleep she would stand by my bedside and fold my hands. Later, though, after Hitler seized power, my father and the whole family left the church and that was it for prayer.

'They haven't helped us,' he said. 'Only the *Führer* has.'

I didn't take religion class anymore and was never

confirmed. I regretted that. At the time there was still stuff to be bought, and Doris got a pile of presents, as well as a confirmation and an examination dress. I complained so long about the unfairness of it all that my mother finally made me a black taffeta dress with white ruffles at the neck and sleeves.

'You've got it good,' said Doris. 'You're getting your confirmation dress for nothing.'

No, I didn't pray right away that night in prison. First I cried, screamed, pounded my fists against the bed. I thought about Jan and the Pole from the railway workshop and about the woman from Rodingen whom Feldmann would have liked to hang right off. I pictured what they were doing to Jan at that moment, or what might already have happened, and what they would do to me; and I thought I would burst, disintegrate right there in the prison cell. And when I couldn't cry any longer and was completely empty and could think of nothing more, I folded my hands and prayed. Help me, dear God, help me out of here. Help Jan. Make them have mercy. Make them not touch him. Make them let him go. Make it possible for him to escape. Make it possible for me to escape. Make them have mercy on me. Make them not touch me. Dear God, help me, help Jan, dear God, you can do it, dear God, save me . . .

I prayed, and my prayer was heard.

Though I don't know if you could call it that. If you could say my prayer was heard and I was saved, when the rescue was such a terrible one. When bombs had to fall on a city, when a couple of hundred people had to die in order for me to be saved.

I lie in the dawn and think it over and would like to know who is right. Gertrud? Or Maurice?

But I was saved.

The attack came unexpectedly. There was no alert, perhaps because the bombers came in too high or because the alert system wasn't functioning. The city was sleeping when it happened.

It went very quickly. I heard a whistle and didn't know at first what the sound meant. Then there was an explosion close by. Then another explosion, and a piece of the ceiling fell in, right behind my bed. I ran into the corner by the cell door, there was another explosion, and half the outside wall fell away. I saw firelight, heard screams, more whistling, another explosion . . .

Suddenly the white-haired guard stood before me.

'Get out!' he said. 'Run!'

I couldn't move.

'Run!' he yelled at me. He took the blanket off the bed, threw it over my head and shoulders, grabbed my hand, and pulled me after him. All around us rubble, breaking walls, flames to one side. He pulled me down a stairwell, along another corridor, into the courtyard. Fire, people, crumbled walls, screaming, running, falling, a man like a torch coming toward us. The guard and I ran on, into the street, to a dark corner behind the cathedral.

'You mustn't go home,' he panted. 'Go somewhere else. Wait.' He took matches and began to singe the ends of my hair, strand by strand.

'There,' he said. 'Now it won't be so noticeable. Still, put the blanket back over you. Run!'

I think I stood there like a stone.

He gave me a push.

'Will you run!'

Then I started moving. With the blanket over my head I ran off, straight ahead, past people who were also running, some half-naked, just as they had pulled themselves from the flames and rubble. I ran and ran. I realized I was on the way home, wanted to turn around, didn't know where to, stopped, ran on. Then I thought of Henninghof. Henninghof at Gutwegen, eighteen kilometers from Steinbergen.

I had often done the distance by bicycle. Now I had to go on foot. They had taken my watch at the prison, but it couldn't be later than two. Eighteen kilometers. I had to make it by dawn.

I wasn't alone. A lot of people were leaving the city, some wrapped in blankets like me, bomb victims on their way to relatives. No one noticed me. I went so fast, I passed them all. By the time I turned off the highway, I was all alone. I began running again, stopped, ran on, thought I saw the dawn, ran faster. It was still dark when I reached Gutwegen. Three hours it took me to do the trip.

I still remember what I thought when I saw Henninghof, the dark house, the wall that surrounds the yard: I've done it. I'm safe. That feeling for the first time since the guard had taken me from my cell. Until then I had just run. The front gate was never locked. I pressed the handle down. The dog barked.

'Harro!' I called softly, and he was still. He knew me. I had fed him often.

I went to the bedroom window of the farmer's wife and knocked.

She stirred, I heard her footsteps. Then the black-out curtain was pushed aside.

'It's me,' I said, and she unlocked the door and let me in. We stood in the front hall, the gray braid fell across her shoulder, her face blurred in the candlelight.

She brought me up to the attic.

'Sleep, Regine,' she said.

That was five months ago. She is dead now. But I am alive. I lie on my bed and breathe and watch the light growing through the window. Perhaps Jan is lying somewhere, too, and breathing. He wakes, he gets up, he dresses, he eats, he drinks, and the time passes for him and for me. Until the war is over.

When the war is over, I'll ride home on Gertrud's bicycle. My mother will cry. Me, too. But not for long. I want at last not to cry anymore.

I know something or other will come.

149

Perhaps Jan will come.

He stands in the doorway, his shoulders drooping forward a bit, with those clear eyes . . . '*Moje kochanie*,' he says.

'Jan,' I say.

'Was it bad?' he asks.

'Now everything is all right,' I say.

We walk through the streets. It is summertime. I have my white dress on.

'At last you can go dancing together,' says Steffens.

And if I don't see Jan again?

'You'll be very sad,' Maurice said on one of the many evenings we sat around the table: 'You'll be very sad, *ma petite*. Until you're happy again.'

'Happy?' I said. 'Without Jan?'

'You're only seventeen,' said Maurice. 'At seventeen I had a girl run off and leave me, and I wanted to throw myself in the Rhône. Later I went fishing in the Rhône. My little son was with me.'

'Someday you'll hold on to your head with both hands,' said Gertrud, 'when you count how many times you've fallen in love.'

She sat there and drank her gooseberry wine, and I said she didn't understand and that if I was never to see Jan again I would rather . . .

'Now just say you'd rather be dead,' said Gertrud. 'Then I'll laugh myself sick.'

She was right. I didn't want to be dead. I wanted to live.

But only with Jan. I was so sure – only with Jan.

And if I never do see him again?

A door slams downstairs. Gertrud is going to the neighbors. She fetches the woman who washes the dead, she lets the preacher know. Soon they will come from all the villages in the area to bury the farmer's wife. A long procession from Henninghof to the Gutwegen cemetery.

I can't go along. But when the war is over, I, too, will walk again through the village. I'll walk to the cemetery and put flowers on her grave.

And if I never do see Jan again?

I lie in the attic and things have changed since last night. Like they did after the bombing raid, when I stood at the window at home and realized I was still alive. Yes, that's what it's like. I'm not afraid anymore; I'm alive, I'll live on; the time will come, something will come for which I'm waiting.

'Lay a path,' Jan had said.

When the war is over, I will begin laying a path.

A NIGHT IN DISTANT MOTION
was set by D E K R Corporation, Woburn, Massachusetts, in Palatino, a typeface designed
by Hermann Zapf. Named after Giovanbat-
tista Palatino, a Renaissance writing master,
Palatino was the first of Zapf's typefaces to
be introduced to America. The designs were
made in 1948; the fonts for the complete face
were issued between 1950 and 1952. The book
has been printed and bound by The Maple-
Vail Book Manufacturing Group, Bingham-
ton, New York. The paper is
Warren's #66 Antique.